MERCY

AN ER THRILLER

RADA JONES MD

APOLODOR

APOLODOR PUBLISHING

Cover design: GermanCreative@Fiverr

Author photograph: Joanna MacLean

ABOUT MERCY

People are dropping like flies in Dr. Emma Steele's ER, and nobody knows why. A new disease? Medication errors? Poisoned oxygen? She must find out, even though her job is in peril, her daughter disappeared, and she'd rather be home, drinking wine.

Is it a mercy killer? But why kill a healthy patient? Is somebody framing her nurses? Or herself?

More strange things happen. A patient's death by stolen medications, her orders corrupted by lethal mistakes, her nurse killed. What happens to her daughter? That's worse than death.

Dr. Steele risks her career and her life to stop the murders. She gets closer and closer to the answers. Until she gets too close.

If you like Patricia Cornwell and Tess Gerritsen, you'll love Rada Jones. Mercy is a fast-paced medical thriller packed with ER action, flawed characters in ever-changing conflict, crisp dialogue, and wine.

PRAISE FOR MERCY

"It was a real page-turner, and I enjoyed it very much! I hope there are more books to come in The Steele Files!"

"MERCY is a delight to read. It's even better than OVER-DOSE. I do love the wine talk. I'm mostly a beer drinker, but reading Mercy almost made me want to rush out and look for those wines. It left me with loads of interesting word images. Definitely a good read!"

"It is fast-paced, and I like all the threads - the ex-husband, the cranky Dr. Ann, the new dog Guinness and the wine of course. I love the commentary of Guinness on his new humans."

"The only problem is, it ended, and all I could think was: No! Don't go! It was clever to add a grownup working dog that thinks as a character."

If there was justice in the world, this book should be dedicated to a dog. Two, in fact.

Gypsy Rose Lee, my shadow, my soul. The world is emptier since you left it. And Kirby, my irreplaceable friend. She adopted us like Guinness adopted Emma, and enriched our lives.

But since most dogs can't read, this book is dedicated to dog lovers.

If you speak to your dog, thinking she understands you, you're on track. If you know she can read your mind, you're with me. If the smile of a dog makes you whole, this book is for you.

ACKNOWLEDGMENTS

My very special thanks to those who made this book possible.

Mauri Rex shook me out of my doctorly jargon so that normal people can enjoy this book. She even remembered the dog food that Emma forgot. She had me remove most "WTF?s" Still, there's plenty left... Thank you, Mauri.

Joyce Jeffrey spent long rainy hours combing through my draft for inconsistencies – there were many – and told me to fix Boris. If you like him, it's because of her. If you don't, it's because of me. Thank you, Joyce.

Joanna MacLean warned me about being "on the nose" with some names and prevented me from giving a villain our friend's name. She was there from the first draft's muddy struggles to the chiseling of the final draft. Thank you, Jo.

And finally, my husband Steve. He suffered through it all, good moods, bad moods and downright disasters. He fought valiantly to eliminate the extra comas and to prevent me from capitalizing fentanyl and propofol. He stuck with me through it all.

For now. But POISON, Book 3, is coming.

MERCY

1

Death: A friend, that alone can bring the peace his treasures cannot purchase, and remove the pain his physicians cannot cure.

Mortimer Collins

Sitting in front of the huge mahogany desk, Dr. Emma Steele hoped her boss would get to the point. This week. She'd been listening to him for ten minutes. An eternity, in ER time. He wasted her time while her patients waited. To distract herself, she imagined him as a worm. She didn't mind being a robin, but eating him? Disgusting. Maybe deep-fried and crusted in Montreal seasoning? With a spicy dip?

"Emma, you know how much I appreciate you," he said, moving the tchotchkes on his desk to avoid her eyes.

She smiled, waiting for "But..." *Nothing before "But..." really matters. It's just lube, helping slide in the message. Like the KY in rectal exams.*

"But your metrics aren't good. The ER costs are going

through the roof. The board grumbles. I can't hold them off much longer."

It's not them. It's you, Emma thought. *You'll throw me under the bus, just to say you're doing something. The metrics can't get better overnight. You know it, but you'll step over me to hold on to your job.*

"I understand."

"You have a month. If your ER's metrics don't improve significantly in a month, I'll have to let you go. I had to pull a lot of strings to give you that, you know. That's all I can do."

"Thanks, Gus."

Dr. Gus Gravelle, vice president of medical affairs of Venice Hospital, nodded without meeting her eyes.

On her way back, Emma checked her watch. *Eight more hours. Today is Vincent's birthday. He'd be nine.* She remembered his red hair, spiking out like a hedgehog. His scent of spoiled milk and baby powder. Her throat tightened. She bit her lip to stop her tears and rushed back to the ER.

2

ANGEL

I hate Mondays. They suck. The noise is deafening. Monitors alarming, phones ringing, drunks cursing. Still, I hear her moaning as I pass by her room. I glance in. She's alone. Screaming.

"Help! Help! Help!"

"What do you need?"

"Help! Help!"

White eyes that used to be green. Thin, greasy hair stuck to her skull. She stinks.

"What can I do?"

"Help! Please! Help!"

"What's your name?"

"Gladys."

"OK, Gladys. How I can help you?"

"Help me!"

She sobs. Tears run down through her deep wrinkles. Her lizard-like hands reach for me.

I step back.

She struggles to sit up. She falls back, screaming.

I grab a pair of gloves to help her up.

She shrieks, burying her dirty nails in me.

I pull away and check my hands. Red crescent marks. That's what I get for helping her.

"Help me."

"I'll be back."

"Don't go, please, don't go."

She wails.

I wash my hands twice. I sign into the EMR, the electronic medical record, looking for her.

There she is. Room 5. Gladys Vaughn, 86. Hip fracture.

I'd like to look inside her record, but I don't dare. Thanks to HIPPA, the patient information protection act, if they catch me I'm screwed.

The computer behind me is on. Whoever used it last didn't log out. Good.

I find her record. She's a wreck. Nursing home. Dementia. Atrial fibrillation. Coumadin.

She's screwed. Her expected mortality is 50 percent per year. She only has a few months. Maybe. Bad ones. She'll hurt when they change her diapers. The flesh of her back will grow holes from lying, rotting in her own urine. It sucks to be her.

I check her orders. A whiff of morphine. Toradol, Tylenol. They won't help much.

I look around. They're all busy, dealing with their own shit.

I go to the break room to get my special vial. I draw it, all five hundred micrograms, in a syringe. It's crystal clear and full. It's happiness in a vial.

I head back. She stares like she never saw me.

"Who are you?"

I smile. "I'm here to help you." I attach the syringe to her IV and push the plunger.

"How's it going, Gladys? Good?"

Her anguish softens. She smiles. Gums only, no teeth. She's happy.

"I know you. You're the Angel."

Me? The Angel? Then it dawns on me.

I'm the Angel of Mercy. I'm the Angel of Death.

I'm the angel.

Her eyes glow.

Then they close.

3

Emma punched in the code to get back in the ER. It was cold. Air conditioners working overtime, as usual. The light, blue and ruthless, was cold too. Emma checked her phone, looking for an answer from Taylor. She hadn't heard from her in two days. That was bad news. *I wonder what she's up to. It's never good.*

She wanted to call her, but she didn't have time. Full stretchers lined the hallways. *Every room must be full.* Monitors beeped, patients moaned, phones rang. It smelled like chlorine and blood. Emma waved her ID over the reader to log into the computer system.

A blood-curdling scream split the heavy background noise. Then another. The circus had started.

Judy, the charge nurse, touched her shoulder.

"Dr. Steele, can you go to Room 1?"

Emma didn't ask why. She threw her stethoscope over her shoulder and headed to Room 1.

Monitors screaming. An old woman. Very old. Cyanotic. Eyes closed. Sharp cheekbones pushing parchment skin. She hasn't had a steak in a while, Emma thought.

She stepped in.

Faith, the nurse, a big, beautiful girl, looked up from placing an IV. The other nurse, Brenda, tiny and brown, killed the alarms.

Emma's nemesis, Dr. Ann Usher, stood at the foot of the bed, watching the resident intubate. She saw Emma and her gray eyes darkened.

The resident, a new one, was bent over the patient. He pushed the laryngoscope blade in the half-opened mouth, moving the tongue out of the way to make room for the endotracheal tube.

The blade is bloody. He's already tried and failed. Maybe more than once.

The RT, respiratory therapist, held the ET tube for him. The alarms screamed. Emma glanced at the vitals. *The blood pressure's low. The oxygen sat is in the 80s. Too low to intubate.*

She moved closer. The RT saw her. His face brightened.

Emma cleared her voice. "You guys need help?"

The resident looked up. The few remaining teeth clicked as they clamped on the blade.

"We're fine, thanks. Let's go!" Ann said, turning her back to Emma.

The alarm got shriller, calling danger.

Oxygen sat 73.

Emma smiled politely. "You may be. The patient is not."

"I can handle this," Ann snarled.

"Of course you can. Can she, though? What's the story?" Emma asked.

Ann crossed her arms. Her lips tightened.

"Nursing home patient. 98. Demented. They sent her here for low oxygen and fever. She had an old DNR, but it wasn't signed," Brenda answered.

Emma looked at Ann. "You think she needs intubation?"

"She'll die without it, doctor!"

"She'll die anyhow. She deserves to die in peace."

"The resident needs to learn. This is a good opportunity. No family, no DNR. It's an excellent case."

Emma's smile vanished.

"She's not a case. She's a person. She deserves comfort and kindness. The resident can learn on other patients."

"She has no DNR. We need to do everything, anyhow. We may as well get something out of it."

"She's 98, demented, and dying. She's not here for our convenience. You have a case for futility. You don't need to do anything but be kind."

Ann's voice rose. "Have you gotten soft? Have you lost your spark? IF you ever had it? I knew they were wrong the day they put you in charge!"

Emma's eyes narrowed, but her voice stayed soft. "She's your patient. It's up to you. I'll review the case. There's nothing that says patients should suffer so that doctors can learn. She'll die, no matter what. Soon. The one thing you can do for her is to give her a good death. Put the patient first. That's the whole point of being a doctor, isn't it?"

Ann grimaced as if she'd stepped in a pile of dog poop. "And you call yourself an emergency physician! You may as well be a psychiatrist."

"What I call myself is not your problem. What you do is."

Her bright red cheeks marring her white face, Ann turned to the resident.

"Thanks to Dr. Emma Steele, our ED director here, we'll just let this patient die. That's how she chooses to practice medicine. I hope you'll do better."

Hands shaking, the resident sat down the laryngoscope. His face flushed, he glanced at the door.

"She needs comfort. Did you give her anything for pain? For sedation?" Emma asked.

He shook his head.

"Try fentanyl. One hundred micrograms to start. Ativan too, if she's still uncomfortable. We don't do things just because we can. When we can't forsake death, we must at least alleviate suffering. That's why we're doctors. We always put the patient first. You understand?"

He nodded.

Poor kid. He'd like a hole to crawl in. There's none. I checked.

Emma left the room. Ann's shrill voice followed her.

"She's totally lost it. She's never been great, but now she's gone out of control. Soon enough she'll start killing them, like Dr. Kevorkian. Stop their suffering, my ass! I can't wait until they get rid of her."

"You'll make a great director, Dr. Usher."

Ann laughed.

Vintage Ann. She must be low on her meds again.

4

Her heart pounding, her throat tight with anger, Emma locked herself in the bathroom to catch a breather. She washed her hands. She looked in the mirror. *What a sight! My face is burning; my heart's racing and my head's about to explode. I want to crush Ann. I want to see her splattered, like a bug on the windshield.*

She took a deep breath. She splashed cold water over her face. Again. Her pulse came down. Her throat softened, and she managed to swallow.

Thank God for bathrooms. That's the only place I can catch a moment to reset. This is nothing but Ann being Ann. She's a good doctor, but what a bitch! She has seniority, so she thinks she deserves to be director. She may even be right. Still, I can't let this go, or I'll lose the respect of the staff. I can't afford that.

Back at her desk, she looked up the patient in Room 1. Ninety-eight. Nursing home. Alone.

I hope I die before I have nothing left to live for. Poor woman. I hope they made her comfortable and let her go.

She went back to running the board, a computer screen lit in every color, displaying the long list of patients, their rooms, their complaints, the staff's comments, the things they waited for. The ultrasound for Room 9 was still pending, but the urine was back on Room 15. *I need to discharge her.*

She finished, just as the speakers coughed their scratchy command: "Code 99, Emergency Department, Room 5."

Emma headed to Room 5. The scrubs parted to let her in.

Room 5, barely big enough for the stretcher and a chair, choked with staff. The rebreathed air was thick with human smells. Dr. Alex Greene ran the code, giving orders. Rudy, the tech, performed CPR. *Good chest compressions. Good recoil, allowing blood return to the heart.*

Like a well-oiled machine, they coordinated without talking. Ben, the nurse assistant director, got a second IV. Sal, the pharmacist, got the drugs. Dr. Greene gave the orders. *They're doing good, but this room is too small.*

"How about moving to a front room?" Emma asked.

"Good idea."

"Room 2's available," Judy said.

Emma nodded.

The doors clanged, opening wide. The stretcher, hidden under the cluster of scrubs like the queen under a clump of migrating bees, rolled to Room 2. Faith bagged. Amy carried the monitor box. Emma and Alex followed.

"What happened?" Emma asked.

"No idea."

"What was she here for?"

"A broken hip. She fell. She looked fine. I called Ortho to admit her. Then, when the nurse went in to check on her, she found her pulseless."

"Who's her nurse?"

"Brenda."

Brenda's good. So's Alex. If there was anything to see, they would have seen it.

The code ran, and ran. Nothing helped. Half an hour later she was still dead. Alex called the code.

Head down, shoulders slumped in dejection, he went to tell the family. He returned looking worse.

"They weren't happy. They don't understand what happened."

"Neither do I," Emma said.

"It makes no sense."

"Heart attack? Stroke? Bleed? Alex, did you scan her head?"

"Come on, Emma. What do you think I am? An intern?"

"Sorry. I'm just trying to understand."

"Me too."

"What did you give her?"

"Not much. A little morphine. Toradol. That's it."

"It didn't look like anaphylaxis."

"No."

"We'll see what the coroner says."

"Don't hold your breath," Alex said.

"I know. I've been here for fourteen years. I'm still waiting for him to offer us something useful." Emma patted Alex's shoulder and returned to her desk.

Between the VPM, Ann's case, and the code, she was behind. Her patients were restless.

She tried to hustle, but something about this case bothered her.

This is the ER. People die all the time. For all sorts of reasons. Some obvious, some not. But this? Going from looking fine to dead, in minutes? That's weird.

She shook her head and went back to work.

It took her a couple of hours to catch up. She took a deep

breath and straightened her back. She sipped on her cold coffee. She shuddered.

She checked her phone. Two missed calls. One unknown number. The other one was Victor.

"Call me."

Emma bristled. *That's all you have to say? Seriously?*

Heart pounding again, she walked to the abandoned radiology reading room. A broom closet really, and just as glamorous. But it was the only place in the ER, besides the bathrooms, where she had privacy. She pulled the accordion doors behind her.

Victor, her ex-husband, was a cardiologist upstairs. He was just as busy as she was, and he wouldn't call without a good reason. The only reason Emma could think about was their daughter, Taylor. And she was never good news.

He answered on the first ring.

"Emma?"

"No, Pope Francis. What's up?"

"Are you at work?"

"Like I'm ever anywhere else."

"Taylor."

"What?"

"She's gone."

"Again?"

"Yes. They haven't seen her since yesterday. They think she left last night."

Emma's heart sank. Taylor was in rehab. *No more.*

"She only had a couple of weeks left. She chose to go there. Why would she do this?"

"She changed her mind?"

"I'm getting tired of this," Emma said.

"Me too."

"Did you try Margret?"

Margret, Victor's mother, was Taylor's favorite person. A modern Southern lady, she drank both tea and bourbon, whenever she saw fit. She looked like a porcelain doll but was as tough as an old saddle.

"I don't want to bother her. She's barely recovered from her heart attack."

"Do you have a choice?"

Victor sighed. "Any other ideas?"

"I'll try Eric." Eric, Taylor's latest acquisition, was a nurse in the ICU.

"If only she was with him," Victor said. "He's a good influence on her."

"He would be, if anyone could influence her worth a damn."

Emma had coped with Taylor, mostly by herself, after Victor left. Taylor had been a difficult child, then a worse teenager. *I thought she was getting it together. Silly me.*

"Emma, don't talk like that. She's doing the best she can."

"She's doing the best she can to drive us crazy, like she's always done." *As usual, Victor is cutting her slack.* Emma's cheeks burned. She wanted to scream. She didn't. *There's no point in us fighting. Not now.*

"I have to go. Why don't you call Margret? I'll find Eric."

6

ANGEL

That was too easy.

They'll never think of me. She wasn't my patient.

I helped the old girl. She'll never suffer again. But I'm running low on fentanyl.

I have to find something else. Quick, painless, untraceable.

Potassium? That burns.

Morphine? That's a controlled substance. It's hard to get.

Insulin? That's easy!

How about a good old pillow? It's quiet. It's free. The old folks won't put up much of a fight. It would be over in a minute. But I need to silence the monitors first. Nobody ever checks, we're all too busy, but you never know.

That's a plan!

Way to go, Angel!

I t was dark by the time Emma got home and dropped her work Crocs at the door. Her bag, heavy with her always-there stuff—scalpel, flashlight, tourniquet, Magill forceps, drugs—went on Victor's old chair, as usual. She bolted the door.

Her wine and the hot bath were the best part of her day. They cleaned her from the dirt and suffering that came with her job. And now that she'd gone off her food to lose weight, they were her only indulgence. She picked her wine carefully. Wine was her solace and her pleasure. It was also half of her daily calories.

Time to celebrate Vincent's 9th.

She settled for an old favorite, Tres Picos 2016, a Spanish Borsao Garnacha. *Most Spanish wines are sharp and full of dark corners, like Goya's paintings. This one is smooth as silk.*

The cork popped, liberating the wine. She poured it in a long-stemmed glass, unfit for the bathtub. She looked through it.

Garnet. Dark enough to appear black, but for the edges. Like venous blood.

She shook her head. *This job's messing with my brain.*

She read the label. "Concentrated flavors of blackberries, strawberries with nuances of leather, vanilla and plums." *Leather? What's leather doing in my wine? Oak is bad enough, but leather? What if I was a vegetarian?*

She sniffed it, then swirled it for the second nose. She took a sip. She chewed on it, bathing all the taste buds. The ones at the back of the tongue, specialized in the bitter taste, and the ones on the sides and underneath. She allowed every single one to revel in the taste, then she swallowed it. It warmed her heart.

She sat on the deep green leather sofa in her scrubs, too tired to take them off. She'd skipped lunch to go see Eric in the ICU. She found him at his post, watching his patients and taking notes. His tired eyes and the five o'clock shadow made him look older than twenty-four. Emma smiled. *Handsome kid! He sure looks better than the first time I saw him, pulseless on that stretcher. I'm so glad I didn't call that code!*

"Hi, Eric."

His face softened when he saw her.

"Dr. Steele! Nice to see you. How can I help you?"

"Have you heard from Taylor lately?"

His eyes widened.

"I visited her just the other day. She was doing great! We had lunch, we walked, we talked."

"Did you have a fight?"

"Fight? Not at all. In fact..." he glanced at his patients, then sighed. He looked back at Emma. "I asked Taylor to marry me. I know she's only seventeen, but she'll be eighteen soon. I really love her. I never felt the way I feel about her. She's the girl of my dreams. I hope you don't mind that I didn't talk to you first, Dr. Steele. I wasn't planning on it. She was so beautiful...and so kind. I couldn't stop."

"What did she say?"

"She cried."

"And then?"

"I told her how much I loved her. I'll wait for her to be ready, no matter how long it takes. There's nobody else for me."

"And?"

"She cried even harder. I gave her my bandanna to blow her nose."

Emma laughed.

"We sat on the grass. We ate ice cream. I told her about the wonderful life we'll build together. I told her that I want her to be the mother of my children. Then she started crying again. I said: 'It's all right. If you don't want children, we'll just get a dog.' I thought she liked dogs. But she cried even harder. Then she ran back in. I think it was the surprise."

"She's pretty young to think about children."

"I know. But she'll get older. I will too."

"Things change. People change. You may not feel the same way next year."

"I will. There is nothing stronger than love."

"How about hate?"

"Hate is love too. Just misguided. Hate is love in disguise."

Emma smiled. "Maybe. Thank you, Eric."

"Why? What happened?"

"Taylor disappeared last night. We don't know where she is. I thought maybe you did."

"Disappeared?"

"Yes. She wasn't in her room this morning."

"But...why?"

"That's what I wondered. Why?" *Now I know.*

This poor girl has got to have cancer. She's bald as a billiard ball, gaunt and yellow. That's chemo. And she's not that old. Forty? Fifty? I look at her patient bracelet. Thirty-three. She got a raw deal. She's holding on to the edge of the stretcher, retching.

I push the second dose of Zofran for her nausea. "How are you doing?"

"Awful. I wish I was dead." She bends over to retch again. "Chemo sucks. And it only buys me a few months anyhow. I wish I hadn't started it. What's the point of living like this? If you can call this life!"

"Why did you do it, then?"

"My parents insisted. I couldn't say no. I didn't know it would be this bad. I'd rather die. It's awful for all of us. They're suffering, watching me die a little every day."

I get it. I'd wish the same if I was her. I need to help her. I have just enough fentanyl left.

On my break, I get the vial from my locker and I head back. Then it dawns on me.

I can't go back. Not yet. Nobody goes back early from their

break. I go to the cafeteria. The stench of grease cuts my breath. I get a cauliflower-cheese soup. It's sickening. I want to puke.

I throw it away, and I go back.

She's gone!

Gone? Did they move her? I check the board. No. She's gone. She got a bed. They took her upstairs. It usually takes hours.

I'm livid. I was going to help her.

I do my circular breathing to calm down. Again. And again. My pulse goes down, and I start thinking straight. I was about to make a huge mistake. She was my patient. If she died, they'd look at me closely. I don't need them looking at me, closely or otherwise.

That was a close call. I was lucky.

Careful, Angel.

Walking in from the ER parking lot that morning, Emma relished the breeze cooling her temples. She'd spent the night wondering about Taylor. Where she was. How she was. At the crack of dawn, she had no answers, but her head throbbed with a massive migraine, complete with nausea and blurred vision. *I hope it starts slow today. I can't even see well enough to suture.*

She punched in the code to open the ER door. The door banged open. The noise hurt her brain.

"Code 66, Emergency Department."

A blue shadow wheezed past. A posse of six followed, all running like the Olympics were on.

Emma followed.

They caught him in the hallway. They grabbed him by the blue paper scrubs. They ripped, exposing abundant pink flesh. Quivering like a hooked fish, he shook them off. He bolted.

They grabbed him again. Carlos pulled on his leg, sending the whole cluster crashing down.

"Let me be, let me be, let me be! You're crushing me. Let me go, let me gooooo!"

Limbs entangled on the concrete floor. Hands grabbed on to body parts. In the wriggling mass of scrubs and bare human flesh, nobody knew who held whom.

"Stay still, damn it!" "Don't bite!" "Ugh, I got his crotch." "Let go, that's my hand!"

"Let me go...let me go...let me go..."

An elderly woman shuffling by on her walker stopped dead, watching. A young mother froze in place, her eyes glued to the fight. Kids screamed. Security came, holding on to their Tasers. The cluster scrambled.

"What a circus," Faith said, watching over Emma's shoulder, her pupils swallowing her eyes.

"Yes. Get me a five-and-two, please. And a stretcher."

The five-and-two, the classic "agitation cocktail" of Haldol and Ativan, was a shot given in the muscle, through clothes if necessary, to sedate dangerous patients.

"Sure."

The fugitive rolled. The hallway melee collapsed again.

"He bit me."

A thump. A scream.

"He broke my nose."

Blood spurted red.

The old lady wavered. A security guard helped her to a chair.

The runaway cried. Strangled, childlike sobs, strange in a man that size. A dozen hands lifted him on the stretcher, holding him there. The fight was over.

"Where's the five-and-two?" Emma asked.

"Here."

Faith grabbed the patient's thigh. She pinched a fold of flesh and cleaned it. In one smooth move, she pulled out the syringe from her pocket, uncapped the two-inch needle with her teeth, plunged it in all the way and pushed the plunger. She pulled it out and recapped the syringe.

Emma shuddered. *What a silly thing to do. A needle stick means weeks, maybe months of testing, prophylaxis, and worry. I need to speak to her.*

"Soft restraints," Emma said.

Judy slid the padded soft cuffs around the patient's ankles and wrists, and tied them to the bed. The man banged his head, crying, but his sobs got softer and softer. Minutes later he was asleep.

The fight was over, but the casualties were heavy. Roy was dizzy and nauseous after hitting his head. Alex's glasses had carved deep gashes into his face before falling apart. Carlos bled from his broken nose. Ben got bitten. His swollen right hand had red tooth marks. The skin wasn't broken, but he was white with anger.

"You! You let go of his leg! That's why he bit me!" He scowled at Carlos.

Carlos wanted none of it.

"Really? He broke my nose because you let go of his hand!"

"I wouldn't have, if you hadn't brought us all down when you pulled on his leg, you stupid spic!"

Carlos turned dark. He charged, ready to punch Ben.

Emma stepped between them.

"That's enough!"

Carlos glared at her. He opened his mouth to speak. He changed his mind. He turned around and left. Ben's narrowed eyes followed him.

Men can't resist a good chase and a fight. You'd think that Alex, at least, would know better than to run after elopers. That's what security is for. Nope. Now I have four extra patients instead of staff. She sent them all to register to get seen, and went to check on Alex's patients, hers now.

Two hours later she came back to find her colleague, Dr. Crump, sitting in her chair. Her heart skipped a beat, then she remembered. *We're friends now. Maybe.* Their long cold war had ended.

"Hi, Emma. I stopped by to finish some charts and I heard you're having trouble. Should I sign in to help for a couple of hours?"

"Really?"

"Why not? I'll just have to be home by five for our anniversary dinner."

"Thanks, Kurt. How's Sheila?"

"She's great. She has gotten younger since we're looking at adopting. It's given her a new lease on life."

"Wonderful. Good luck." Emma smiled.

Why on earth do people want children? Like life isn't hard enough without them. I should lend them Taylor. They'd get over it real fast.

Hours later, when her shift was almost over, Emma went to recheck the chest pain in Room 14. She turned the corner and walked into Faith. *I need to speak to her about that needle. I may as well do it now.*

"Faith, you have a moment?"

"Sure..."

"Let's go for a walk."

They walked out through the EMS entrance in the back. After the raw electric lights in the ER, the sun was a loving caress. The air was soft, the shadows long, the light golden. The scrawny bushes in the parking lot glowed, unfurling raw green leaves. Spring had finally come.

Emma inhaled the scent of moist, rich earth. Outdoors, she felt free. She looked at Faith and smiled. Faith looked away. *She's worried. She must be busy, and I'm slowing her down. Or maybe she thinks she's in trouble.*

"Thanks for your help with that patient. I know he wasn't yours."

"Of course. We're a team. I'm glad to help."

"You did. There's something I need to tell you though."

Faith stepped away.

"I'm concerned about you recapping that needle. Please don't do that. If you get stuck, you can get HIV, hepatitis, God knows what other diseases that we don't even know about yet. I don't want you to get hurt."

Faith sobbed. Emma felt like she'd hit a puppy.

"I'm sorry, Faith. I didn't mean to upset you. I just want you to be safe."

Tears started down Faith's cheeks. Emma touched her shoulder. "Faith, are you OK?"

"Yes."

"Something's troubling you?"

Faith shook her head, and her silky golden hair surrounded her like an aura.

"What's going on, Faith?"

"I've been emotional lately. Ever since I lost my father."

"I'm sorry. I heard about that. It must be hard for you."

"I was away for a month, taking care of him. It wasn't a good death. He had cancer."

"That must have been awful."

"It was. He was in excruciating pain all the time. Day and night. The cancer metastasized to his ribs. They broke. The pain was so bad that he screamed every time he took a breath."

"That's horrific. How come he didn't get better pain control?"

"He refused. He didn't want to die addicted. He said God was trying him before taking him to heaven. He wanted to be worthy."

"I'm sorry." Emma touched Faith's shoulder.

"Mother and I, we got to watch him suffer. It was hard for her!"

"It must have been hard for you, too."

"It was. It took him weeks to die."

"How are you doing?"

"I'm getting by," Faith sobbed.

Emma looked around for a quiet spot. She remembered the family room, the small private space dedicated to families waiting for news about their critically ill loved ones. She took Faith there. They sat side by side on the cheap vinyl sofa. Emma took Faith's hand.

"What's going on, Faith? You miss your father?"

Faith laughed.

"Oh, no. I don't miss him. Just the opposite. He was a horrible man. He beat me for everything, ever since I was barely old enough to walk. He was not a good man."

Emma patted Faith's arm. *What do I say now? I'm glad he's dead?*

"I'm so sorry."

"It's not about my father. It's about Carlos."

"Carlos?"

"Yes. My fiancé."

Of course. Faith and Carlos are an item. They came together from New Hampshire a few months ago. I forgot.

"Don't worry, his nose will heal in no time! The new ENT is excellent! He'll make Carlos even more handsome than before!"

Faith shook her head. "It's not that. He left me."

"Carlos left you?"

"Yes. He moved out. After my father died, I came back to an empty place."

"That's awful!" Emma hugged her.

Faith clung to her, hugging her so tight that she could hardly breathe.

"He must be stupid to leave you. You're so beautiful, and

so talented. Maybe he just needs time to sort himself out. I bet he'll be back."

Faith let go. She blew her nose.

"He won't be back."

"Why not?"

"I have...I have done things that he can't forgive."

"You never know."

Faith shook her head.

"If he came back, would you take him?'

Faith looked at her with unblinking blue eyes.

"I don't know. But he won't come back." She headed to the door. "Thank you, Dr. Steele."

Emma wished she could help.

"Faith? How about meeting somewhere for a coffee and a chat?"

Faith's face lit up. "When?"

Too late, Emma wished she'd kept her mouth shut. *I need socializing like I need a hole in my head. Shit. I just couldn't see this nice girl suffer without trying to help.*

"Thursday?"

Faith nodded. She left smiling.

Emma sighed. *I'm just selfish and lazy. Who knows? It may even be fun!*

11

Taylor had walked for hours. The rehab building had to be miles behind. She looked back. Nothing. No trace of humanity. Nothing but trees, birds, and bees. All having a good time. All, but her. She shrugged under the weight of her backpack. Her shoulders hurt. She rolled them, but it didn't help. She was tired, but she didn't dare come out yet.

I'm too close. They must be looking for me. If they find me, they'll drag me back.

She drank a little water and tightened her waist strap, loading more of the weight on her hips. It was a bright spring morning; warm enough to make her jacket feel like extra weight rather than comfort. She unzipped it to let the breeze in. *I'll walk through the woods for another hour, and then I'll head to the road.*

She was tired and she hurt. More than anything, she was pissed. Really pissed. Her mother was right. Again.

"You can't do that, Taylor. You have to tell him."

"Why?"

"He'll find out. He'll feel betrayed and lose trust in you. You can't build a relationship on lies. It doesn't work!"

"Like you know a lot about relationships!"

Emma took in that quick sharp breath that told Taylor she'd hit the mark. Touched her right where it hurt. Then she smiled.

"I know more than you do. I know how to make them, and I know how to break them. But this isn't about me, it's about you. You need to tell him."

"Maybe. Maybe not. If I tell him now, he'll run away. He may never come back. If I wait, he may care enough to want me, no matter what. Plus, I may never need to tell him. Shit happens. He may be nowhere close by the time I start showing."

"He's a decent person, Taylor. I don't think he'll go away. If he does, he does. That's life. You can't pretend to be somebody you're not. Not for long. He'll find out, and it will be worse."

"I can tell him it's his."

"That's silly. First of all, he'll know. He's a nurse. You're almost four months pregnant. How are you going to explain a full-term baby born at six months? He'll know. So will everybody else. Second, the idea itself is appalling. You can't lie to him like that! Third, the real father knows. What if he comes back?"

"He won't come out for a long, long time. I'll cross that bridge when I get to it."

"What if the baby isn't normal?"

"Eric knows I'm going into rehab. He knows the risks of doing drugs while you're pregnant."

Emma gave up. There was no convincing Taylor. She had made up her mind.

Until the other night. Eric was so sweet! He looked at her

as if she hung the moon. He'd do anything for her. She could tell him the baby was his, and he'd believe her. She could tell him the truth. He may run away. He may not. Not because of the baby. Because of the lie, like her mother said.

She had looked in his eyes. She'd wanted to tell him: "I'm pregnant. We've already started a family."

She couldn't. She ran away instead, looking for a hole to hide in. So she planned her escape.

She spent a day getting ready. She could either carry some weight, or she could walk far. Not both. She left most of her stuff behind. She took her computer, her jacket and a flashlight, plus water, cookies, and all the dry fruit she could find.

She left before daybreak. She tiptoed out, then walked to the back fence. She climbed up the leaning oak tree she'd scoped the day before. She dropped her pack over the fence and looked down. The ground was far away.

She remembered something she had read about African women.

They abort by jumping off trees. Gravity pulls the placenta away from the uterus, killing the fetus. If I lose this pregnancy, I'd never have to tell him. Then I could have his child instead.

She looked up. Another branch, six feet higher. *That should do it.* She started climbing.

I can't do this. I just can't.

She climbed back down to the lowest branch. She grabbed it, dangling as low as she could. She let go softly, breaking her fall on bent knees. She rolled over to dissipate the energy, like she'd seen in movies.

She stood up. Her shoulder hurt. She'd caught a rock. She pushed on her belly with her hands. It didn't hurt. She put on her pack, then she walked, and walked. To where? She wasn't sure.

I'd like to go to Grandma. She'll be happy to have me. But that's the first place they'll look. I could go to New York City. They'll never find me there. But I don't have much money. Only enough for a few days. Then what? I'll go to Katie. She won't tell. I'll be safe there while I get it together.

Her back hurt. Her belly started hurting too. A cramp scrunched her over. She stopped to catch her breath. She started again.

Another one. Longer. She checked her watch.

I need to walk for another half an hour.

A third cramp took her breath away.

She didn't have another half an hour. She needed a ride. Now.

To where?

She sat, hugging her knees. She took slow, even breaths.

Something's wrong with the baby. It looks like I'm losing it, after all. Where should I go?

The pain in her heart hurt more than the cramps in her belly. She took out her phone and checked the map. The road was half a mile to her left. She took another sip of water and headed there.

A cramp cut her at the knees. She lay down in the young green grass, moist with dew.

I'll totally ruin my jacket. Another cramp. She gathered her knees to her chest and lay on her side in the fetal position. She waited. The cramps stopped.

She got her pack and headed to the road, crushed by the weight, the pain, and her guilt.

12

B ack in the ER for another shift, Emma was reading Room 5's EKG when Kurt stopped by.

"Emma, you have a moment?"

Resplendent, as always, in his dark suit and tie, he made her feel shabby. Her bleached scrubs were too tight. And dirty. *They were clean this morning,* she thought, hoping the brown spots on her thigh were coffee rather than somebody's body fluids. "Sure."

"Can you look at a rash?"

"I'm lousy with rashes, but I'll do my best."

"Room 20. Failure to thrive. She doesn't look well, and she's got blisters in her mouth. I'm worried about Stevens-Johnson syndrome."

"I haven't seen that in ages. I hope you're wrong," Emma said. Stevens-Johnson, one of the few dermatological emergencies, started with a rash and ended with the skin peeling off in sheets.

The woman in Room 20 was hard to look at. She was small and frail. Her cracked lips were bloody, her eyes glued shut.

Emma turned on her flashlight. *Blisters. On her neck, on the palate, on the tongue. Herpes?* "Does it hurt?"

"Not much," the woman slurred.

"Maybe it's not herpes then. That sucker hurts like a son of a gun! Kurt, I'd call Infectious Diseases. I'd treat her for sepsis. Fluids, antibiotics, bring her in."

"Thanks, Emma."

"I hope you feel better soon," Emma said. She glanced at the old man sitting by the door leaning on his cane. "We'll do our best to help her."

"Thank you." He smiled, looking behind Emma's shoulder.

Her heart sank. *He's blind. How will he manage without her? There's nothing worse than losing one's life partner. Except for losing a child.*

She touched his shoulder, wishing she could help, and went back to her patients. Back pain in Room 12.1. Depression in Room 7. Sepsis in Room 10.

She was just telling the back pain that she can't give him Percocet if he's allergic to Tylenol, when the speakers croaked: "Code 99, Emergency Department, Room 20."

She went to help. The room was already full. Gail performed CPR. Carlos bagged. Dozens of busy hands placed IVs, attached monitors, pushed meds. Kurt was ready to intubate.

Emma prepared his tube. She glanced at the patient to choose a tube size. She recognized the bloody dry lips. *That's the patient Kurt had me see. She wasn't that bad. What happened?*

Kurt ran the code like the pro he was. It made no difference. The patient stayed dead.

Half an hour later, Kurt called the code. Everybody went

back to their work. Everybody, but the blind elderly husband. He sat by the bed holding the blue hand.

Emma's heart cried for him. She looked for Kurt.

"What happened?"

He shrugged. "I don't know. I gave her fluids and antibiotics. She looked better. When I went back to check on her, I found her dead."

"Weird!"

Kurt nodded, his lips a tight line.

"A heart attack maybe? A stroke?"

"I don't know."

"Anaphylactic reaction to antibiotics?"

"It didn't look like it. No hives, no swelling, she was bagging all right...It makes no sense," Kurt said.

"That's odd."

"It sure is. It will be a coroner's case."

"Don't hold your breath."

Emma didn't understand what happened, and that drove her crazy. *Things don't happen without a reason. She died out of the blue, only a couple of hours after I saw her. She looked all right. Then Bam! She's dead. Why? Even worse, she's not the first one. The first one was the hip fracture in Room 5. Just like this one. OK now, dead an hour later. For no reason. Something isn't right... But what? A bad batch of medications? The oxygen? Some weird communicable disease we don't recognize?*

Emma hated things she didn't understand. She lived to fix people. That was her only skill. *I'm a lousy mother, I failed as a wife, I can't sing or draw or play sports. The one thing I'm good at is being a doctor. Now I'm failing at that too. I'd better figure it out soon.*

Before it strikes again.

13

T hat was easy.

Poor woman! The rash! Those bloody lips!

I left to get my fentanyl, when I saw the insulin sitting on the counter. I grabbed it.

"What is it?" she asked.

"Something to make you feel better."

"Thank you. Can I have some water?"

I brought her water. I brought some for her husband too.

"What's your name?" she asked.

"Angel."

"You are an angel," he said.

The poor man is blind. He can't take care of her. She must be taking care of him. What will he do without her? I hate to separate them, but she needs relief. I wish I could send them together, but I can't. Two deaths in one room? That's overkill. Except for carbon monoxide. That would kill them both. I'd have to close the door. But there are detectors. And how do I get carbon monoxide? Not like I can get a car in here.

Cyanide? Mushrooms? I need to think.

Next time.

14

E mma signed out her last patient and headed upstairs. Her rotten shift was finally over. She couldn't wait to go home. She had to find Taylor. She needed wine. And a hot bath.

Instead of that, she went to meet Carlos, like the VPM had asked her to. Carlos wanted Ben fired. He threatened to sue the hospital. Emma was supposed to talk him out of it. *Fat chance.*

She stepped in the windowless conference room. Carlos waited, alone but for the dismembered intubating mannequins piled in a corner. Bald heads attached to limbless torsos. Rubber faces with toothless gaping mouths. Glazed eyes staring into nothing.

But for his arms and legs, Carlos could be one of them.

Death awaits.

The thought came out of nowhere. Foreboding poisoned the air. Emma shuddered. She needed to get out.

"Let's go to my office."

Carlos followed. He sat across her desk, staring at his hands.

"What's happening, Carlos?"

He shifted in his chair, his bruised eyes avoiding her.

"What's up, Carlos? You started so well. Everybody loved working with you. Always patient, smiling, ready to help. Then you changed. People complain that you've been short lately. What's going on?"

"You were there, Dr. Steele. You heard him."

"Carlos, there's more to it than that. You've been struggling for a while."

Carlos shivered.

"Are you sick?"

"I need to grab a candy bar. I skipped lunch. My sugar must be running low."

Emma handed him her power bar. Her mouth watered. *I don't need it anyhow. I'm heading home.*

"You're diabetic?"

"Since I was twelve." He unwrapped it and took a bite. He struggled to chew. His face was bruised, his thick nose crooked. He finished, rolled the wrapper into a ball and put it in his pocket.

"Thank you." His eyes, black holes, met Emma's. She shivered.

"Carlos, is this about Faith?

"How do you know?"

"She told me. I'm sorry for both of you. It must be hard."

"It is. I had nowhere to go. I slept in my car, until George took me in."

"He's a good man. I'm glad he's your friend."

"Me too."

"You think it's all over with Faith?"

"Yes. Faith did things I can't forgive. I said things she can't forget. It's over."

"It must be hard to work together."

"They don't put us on the same team."

"Let me know if I can help."

Carlos nodded, his hunched shoulders spelling defeat.

It's sad, but he'll get over it. He's young, he's smart, he's handsome. She will too. It just takes an awful long time. Even after love dies, it still hurts.

"About Ben."

Carlos turned red. "Fucking Jew!"

"Come on, Carlos! How is this better than what he called you?"

"He's not here to hear it. And he started it."

"Carlos, we're not in kindergarten. We're grown-ups. We work together like professionals. We respect each other."

"Is this how he behaved? Grown up?"

"No. That's why he got demoted. He lost his position as assistant director. He got a warning. He'll have to go through sensitivity training."

"And you think that's enough? Dr. Steele, do you have any idea what it took for me to get here?"

"No, Carlos, I don't. Tell me."

"I was a street kid from Puerto Rico. My father? I don't even know his name. My mother worked three jobs to feed my brother and me. She was never home. I was twelve when I joined the gang. I was fourteen when I went to juvie. Do you have any idea how hard it was to get myself together? To get my GED? To go to college? I got my degree working nights as a janitor. I walked dogs. I went hungry. For eight fucking years. I did whatever it took to pull myself together and never go back. And now this fuck calls me an incompetent spic?"

"You just called him a fucking Jew. What do you know about his life?"

Carlos glowered. "I know plenty. He's got an ugly past. I know. I was there for some of it. I heard about the rest. One of these days...One of these days I'm going to talk, no matter what. It's worth it, just to see him fall apart."

"Carlos, you need to stop. You won't throw away all your hard work just because he called you names? You're smarter than that, Carlos. I hope you are."

Carlos shook his head. He stood up and headed to the door.

"Good night, Dr. Steele."

Driving home, Emma wondered what that meant. *It's none of your business, leave me alone? Or is it: I'll think about it?*

She pulled in the garage. She dropped her Crocs, walked in the kitchen, and dropped her bag.

I need wine to warm me up inside. 19 Crimes, 2017 Shiraz, South Eastern Australia. "British rogues, guilty of one of nineteen crimes, were sentenced to transportation. This wine celebrates the rules they broke and the culture they built." The wine reminded her of Carlos. She opened the bottle and poured the dark ruby wine in a tall glass. She inhaled. *Almost black. Rich aroma. Dark fruit. A hint of honey.* Her mouth watered. She lifted the glass.

She heard a sound in the house. She froze. She put down the glass. Head up, chin forward, she listened. Nothing. *The pipes? The heat? A burglar?*

She crept to her bag and grabbed the scalpel. *It won't do much against a gun, but that's the best I've got.* She slid toward the living room.

The noise again.

She blew the door open. Taylor froze.

"Taylor?"

"Mother?" Taylor laughed.

Emma saw herself through Taylor's eyes. *A scared, overweight, middle-aged woman in dirty scrubs threatening the world with a scalpel. Move over, Hitchcock!*

"Welcome home, Taylor."

Emma was late on Thursday for her date with Faith. They planned to hike Silver Lake Mountain, and Emma couldn't find a pair of hiking pants that fit. She ended up with a pair of maternity pants she hadn't worn since Vincent. She pulled her red Hyundai next to Faith's black Chevy pickup, wondering about her taste in cars. She knew some girls loved tractors, but a truck?

They headed up the path, Faith first. Emma scrambled behind her trying to keep up. She hadn't hiked in years. Ever since she'd chaperoned Taylor's class in seventh grade. It hadn't been much fun.

The other parents bragged about their kids' soccer goals, violin concertos, and volunteering. Emma wasn't into bragging. She didn't have much to brag about, either. "Taylor's doing great. She hasn't killed anyone yet. That we know of." Fortunately, nobody asked her anything. They only talked about themselves and their kids. As usual, she listened.

Faith's orange leggings moved swiftly, sidestepping boulders and puddles. She made it look easy. Emma scrambled behind her, watching her feet. The trail was uneven and muddy. She had already slipped twice.

She'd never talked to Faith outside work. Not much at work, either. *There's no time to chat in the ER. And if you ever do, it's at 4 a.m., after the evening rush dies down. For an hour or so. By six, the heart attacks start coming. By seven, the nursing homes find those who died overnight. By eight, the hangovers stop by for work notes, and by nine you're back in business.*

She was hungry for air. She stopped to catch her breath, pretending her boots needed tightening.

I wish we had gone for a pedicure instead. Too late now. It's a small hike. Less than a mile. How bad can it be?

Faith waited.

"You have kids?" Emma asked, making conversation.

Faith shook her head. A tear ran down her cheek.

Do I know how to break the ice or what? Her parents are another minefield. So is Carlos.

"They're seriously overrated. You can have mine if you want her."

Faith's periwinkle eyes widened. She laughed. "What's wrong with her?"

"I'd tell you, but we don't have the whole day. You want kids?"

"I always wanted kids. Carlos didn't. And...the other men in my life didn't either." Faith shrugged. "Too bad. I know I would be a good mother. I didn't want to have a kid whose father didn't want him. My own childhood was bad enough."

"I'm sorry about that. Mine wasn't that great either."

"Was it your father?"

"No, he died when I was a baby. My mother was mentally ill."

"Lucky you!" Faith said.

Emma laughed. Faith blushed.

"I meant you're lucky that your father wasn't mean to you. That came out awful."

"Funny though. What was wrong with your father?"

"He was a religious nut. Everything had to be done by the Bible. I couldn't start the microwave without praying first."

"I didn't know they mentioned microwaves in the Bible!"

"They did, in my father's. That's why they named me Faith. It was either that or Genesis."

"You were lucky."

"I guess."

The stony path got steeper and steeper. The trail became an irregular rock stairway heading straight up toward the sky. Emma had trouble putting one foot in front of the other. Her heart pounded fasted and faster. She ran out of air. She felt faint.

She stopped to rest. She drank water. Faith waited.

Emma looked up. A stairway to heaven. She looked down. Between the branches, she caught a glimpse of blue water, far below.

"We'll have a beautiful view when we get there," Faith said.

If we get there.

"How much further, you think?"

"We're about halfway, but it gets steeper toward the end."

"Doesn't it always?" Emma spat.

Faith laughed. "Just like the night is darkest just before dawn."

"Have you been here before?"

"Last winter. Carlos loves the outdoors. We used to hike,

bike, and kayak together in New Hampshire. Here too, until..."

"I've heard New Hampshire is beautiful. I've never hiked there," Emma said, trying to change the subject.

"Do you really think Carlos will come back?"

Emma stopped to breathe. She could hike, or she could talk. Not both. *She chats like she's window shopping, while I'm dying. But she's ten years younger, and in amazing shape. Not me.*

"I do. People need time to understand themselves. They come, they go, they wiggle. It's hard to get together. It's hard to break apart. But the question is: should you take him back?"

"It's hard to be alone."

"I know. Were you happy with him?"

"Not when he drank. He got angry."

"He's a mean drunk?"

"Aren't they all?" A shadow passed through Faith's limpid eyes. "Why do I always get involved with nasty men?"

"Faith, you're so young. You're beautiful and vibrant! You'll find a man who deserves you. You have time to have children, if that's what you need."

"I loved Carlos."

"You still do?"

"I don't know. He's comfortable. He's safe. He's home." Faith slowed down as she climbed the last dozen rough steps. "Change is hard," she said softly.

Emma nodded, too winded to talk.

"But it's necessary. Like iron forged in fire, we all have to go through the events that will shape us into the people we need to become," she declared.

Too tired to care, Emma followed her to the top. Far, far below, Silver Lake glimmered in the morning sun. Covered in pine trees, the mountains were dark blue but for the white snowcaps. The blue sky stretched forever. The beauty filled Emma's heart with joy.

She grabbed her phone to take pictures and stepped forward to avoid a tree branch.

A rock rolled under her foot. She slipped. The other foot followed. She slid, feet first. She reached for the tree branch. She missed. She hit the ground, sliding down. Nothing ahead but the lake. A mile away.

The void smiled.

She wished she'd been a better mother. A better doctor. A better person.

The void called.

She tried to grab the ground. The rocks rolled with her.

The void sucked her in.

She stopped.

Faith had grabbed her. Holding her hood with one hand, a tree branch with the other, she dragged her back.

They fell back on the trail.

The lake sparkled. The sun bathed the mountains as if nothing had happened.

Nothing had.

"Thank you, Faith."

Faith smiled, her eyes bluer than the sky above.

"Of course. That's what friends do."

Emma's eyes burned.

It's good to have friends.

16

Carlos needed his stuff. Faith was at the hospital. He'd just grab his stuff and go.

He climbed the old sloping staircase and unlocked the door. The spotless kitchen felt foreign. *She must be pleased I'm no longer here to leave a mess. I'll get in and out before she gets back.* He propped the door open with a boot. He got her those boots. *That was before...*

He shook his head to banish the thought. His boxes were in the spare room. He grabbed two and took them to the car. Three trips later, the car was full.

I'll come back for the rest.

He took a last look around. Faith's faded pink robe hanging on the door. Her ER Pearls book, open on the coffee table. Her slippers, shaped like her feet. Nothing of his, but the picture of the day he proposed. Him, kissing her. Faith, smiling, looking at his ring.

I wonder if she still has it.

He headed to the door just as Faith stepped in. Her beauty took his breath away, as always. Her golden hair, alive with movement. Her indigo eyes sparkling against her flushed cheeks. She smiled.

She's not surprised.

"I was expecting you, but I thought you'd call first."

"I didn't want to bother you."

"How considerate! I never get to see you, these days. Sit."

"I need to go."

"Why the big rush?"

Faith stood in the door, blocking it. Carlos sighed.

"Is this how you treat old friends? You come in like a burglar and leave without saying good-bye? What's wrong with you, Carlos?"

"You know damn well, Faith. There's nothing wrong with me."

"You think there's something wrong with me?"

"Come on, Faith. There's no point in opening old wounds!"

"Oh, but there is, my friend. I miss you."

"I don't miss you. And you're lying. You don't miss me. You miss him!"

"I miss him too. But he's gone. You're here!"

Carlos shook his head. He tried to get past her.

She grabbed him. She held him close, lifting her beautiful rose mouth to his. Her perfume, honey, jasmine and moist earth, enveloped him. His knees weakened.

He tried to disengage. She clung to him. His knees gave.

They fell on the floor. Her lips found his. Her tongue tasted him.

He forgot to resist. She slowly, lovingly, opened his buttons. She kissed his face, sucked on his earlobe, breathed short hot breaths under his chin. She stroked the place between his legs where his brain had melted.

He forgot everything: Dick, the car in the driveway, George waiting for him with a beer. He forgot everything but Faith. Her scent, imprinted in his soul. Her moist mouth, hot in the open zipper of his jeans. He hurt in the beauty of the feeling. Nothing else mattered. He was whole.

17

Emma punched the ER silver door opener and flew in through the door. She'd been upstairs, in the hospital, assisting with a code. *Like I don't have enough to do in the ER. I've been away from my patients for half an hour. That's insane. Any doctor should be able to manage that.* She huffed, rushing to her desk.

Kurt was waiting in her chair.

"You care for a walk?"

Like I care for an STD.

She checked the board. Five new patients waiting to be seen. Plus all the others.

"Now?"

He nodded.

They walked out through the ambulance door. Walking from there to the main entrance gave them three minutes of privacy. Five, if they stopped to tie their shoes. Eyes and cameras were everywhere, watching, but they couldn't hear.

"That death, the other day..."

"Yes."

"It was hypoglycemia."

Low blood sugar? "How low?"

"Her blood glucose was 12."

Twelve? How can that be? Normal is 90 or so. At 60 they get weird. Lower, they seize and behave like a stroke. How could Kurt miss that?

"Was she a diabetic?"

"No. And before you even ask: we had already checked her glucose. It was normal!"

"How did you find out?"

"I have friends."

The coroner's office.

"How could that happen?"

"I'm wondering if she got insulin. The next-door patient, Room 21, was a diabetic with a glucose in the 500s. I ordered 30 units of insulin for him. What if she got it instead?"

"That would be a huge mistake. "

"Shit happens. With all the interruptions, I'm surprised we don't make more mistakes."

"You checked your orders?"

"I did. They were correct. Still, the nurse may have given it to the wrong patient."

"But they have to check the patient's ID first."

"They would. Unless they got distracted. I don't know what happened, but I thought I'd warn you. This is going to come out, and we won't look pretty."

"Nope. Can you think about any other scenario?"

"I can't. It's got to be the insulin."

Damn. That's exactly what I needed.

Emma's job hung from a thread. The ER metrics had been bad for years. To fix them, the hospital had fired all the docs and hired a contract group. Fortunately, the group took them on. Emma became director. They told her to improve the metrics and lower the costs. Soon. Or else. She hadn't.

I'm screwed. Even if it's a nursing error, and the nurses are Mike's responsibility, not mine, Gus will drop me faster than a hot potato. Ann is waiting in the wings to take my job. Oh well. It was good while it lasted.

The heck it was. This job sucks. Being director is not doctoring. It's politics. Filthy business. It sucks to fail. But it would be awesome to no longer be on call. And tell them all to fuck themselves. I get five job offers a day. In places more exciting than this. I could go to Australia, where they have kangaroos. Or to New Zealand. They have penguins. I love penguins!

Back at her desk, smiling wide, she logged into the system. Ann stared as she passed by. Emma waved.

I can't wait to see you on call 24/7. Fucked from above and from below. It's all worth it, right there.

Ann frowned.

Emma laughed. *I wish they could transplant a sense of humor. It would do Ann a world of good.*

By the time she got home that evening, Emma was "hangry". So hungry, she was angry. She had nothing but coffee all day. After February, she decided to do something for herself. She was going to lose those extra pounds. Easier said than done. Her schedule sucked. The break room overflowed with junk food. Only one way to do it: stop eating at work. No doughnuts, no cake, no junk.

This way I can enjoy my wine without worrying about calories.

Her hands were shaky and her fuse was short, as she dropped her bag on the chair. Taylor was obviously better. The sink was full of dirty dishes.

Why does she need a new dish every time she takes a bite? Because she doesn't do the dishes, that's why!

Emma hated dirty dishes. In her private list of least favorite things, dirty dishes were #2. After rats, and before stepping in dog poop. Snot was #4, but that came with the job. Dishes didn't. It took all she had to control her OCD and ignore the sink.

Hip-hop music thundered from Taylor's room, jarring Emma's empty stomach. Taylor lay in bed, reading the second Harry Potter. The book was falling apart.

She's been crying again. That smudged mascara makes her look like a raccoon.

"How are you?" Emma asked.

"OK. You?"

"Better now that I'm home. How are you feeling?"

"Same, same."

"Any bleeding?"

"Not yet." Tears streamed down her thin face.

Emma's soul hurt. She wanted to hug her, but she knew better. *She's like a cat. She only wants to be touched when she's ready. Not now.*

"How's the pain?"

"Same. Cramps every fifteen minutes."

"You want to go get checked?"

Her softness vanished.

"I told you no! Five times!"

"I thought you changed your mind."

"I never change my mind!"

Emma laughed. *Not more than every five minutes, you don't.* Taylor understood and broke in a rare smile.

"Not that often. I'll find out soon enough anyway."

"But..."

"You said there's no way to prevent a miscarriage. If I get worse, you'll take me there."

"Don't you want to know?"

"I'm afraid to find out. I don't want to know. Well, I do, but only if it's good news."

"What's good news for you?"

Taylor frowned.

"What do you mean? I see. If I miscarry, I don't need to

tell Eric." She cupped her growing belly between her hands. "Good news would be to see the baby alive. I can't wait to hold him. But I don't know how to tell Eric."

"You'll have to make a decision."

"Not now. I have enough on my plate.

Not really. You lie in bed, wallowing in self-pity. You read Harry Potter. You wonder what's happening but don't want to know.

"Your father and Eric are sick with worry. You need to tell them you're OK."

"I will, eventually."

"When?"

"When I'm ready."

"When are you going to be ready?"

Taylor sat up. Dark hair streamed around her narrow face like hissing snakes.

The harpy woke up.

"I'll let you know. Now, if you don't mind…"

"I mind. You need to tell them."

"It's my business. I'll tell them when I'm ready!"

"It's my business too. This is my house. You chose to come here."

"I needed help. I trusted you!"

"I let you be long enough. You tell them or I will. By tomorrow."

"Are you serious?" Taylor's pale cheeks flushed with anger.

"Damn serious. Get out of the hole you dug for yourself. You shouldn't have lied to Eric…"

"I didn't lie to Eric! I never said a lie!"

"You lied by omission. You know what you did. I told you then that it was a bad idea. You didn't listen. You never do. If you don't tell them, I will. It's up to you."

"Mother!" Taylor sobbed. "Please, you can't do that…"

Miss Bipolar is working on me. She'll do whatever it takes! If anger didn't do it, pity will. No, baby, we've already played this game too many times. I'm not your father, who always lets you have your way. Nor poor Eric.

"Taylor, I'm helping you become a responsible adult. You have until tomorrow. If you don't call Eric and your father, I will."

19

Carlos woke up in Faith's bed. She was warm and soft, and she smelled like chocolate, pepper, and sex. He luxuriated in her scent. Until the memories exploded in his brain.

She enticed him. He surrendered.

She broke down his defenses. Again. He forgot that she cheated on him, betrayed him and uprooted his life. Once again, he fell for her. As soon as she touched him, he melted into a haze of lust. He was her toy. She called, and he dropped everything. He had left his life possessions in the street.

He saw red. He was angry at her, but even angrier at himself. She had wrapped him around her finger. Again.

He struggled to control his breath. He slid out of the bed with less noise than a falling feather. He crept to the kitchen. His clothes were on the floor. No underwear. He pulled on his pants and T-shirt, grabbed his jacket, and snuck out like a thief.

Get out before she ensnares you again.

The last two boxes sat by the door, where he'd dropped

them. He wanted to take them, but couldn't take the risk. He slipped through the door, leaving it open. He took the steps as if he stepped on hot nails.

The trunk was empty. So was the car. Every single box was gone. His tools and his bag too.

He spat his anger to the ground and took off without closing the trunk. Anything to not wake her up. He deserved to lose his stuff. He'd been stupid.

Never again.

I won't come back.

20

Sitting across the desk in Mike's office, Emma struggled to keep her cool. She had stopped by to talk to him on her way to the ER, but he didn't want her there. He didn't say it, but his eyes avoiding hers and his sullen expression were loud enough.

Too bad. We need to talk.

The coroner's report was out. Hypoglycemia.

"Why would she be hypoglycemic? She wasn't diabetic. She wasn't ordered insulin. She wasn't even septic."

"We'll do a root cause analysis," Mike said.

"Could it be a medication error? We need to test for C-peptide. That will tell us if she received any insulin."

Mike cleared his throat.

"We're still waiting for some of the results."

"Did we test for C-peptide?"

Mike looked at his watch.

"I don't see how that makes a difference."

"There was no insulin order for her. If she received any, that would make it a nursing error."

"There could be a verbal order," Mike said.

"Why? She wasn't hyperglycemic. There was no reason to give her insulin!"

"Her potassium was high. Maybe they gave it for high potassium."

"5.2 isn't that high. If they gave insulin for that, they should give glucose too. And there's still no order."

"As I said, we'll do a root cause analysis. We'll talk to pharmacy and risk management."

"I think it's a nursing error."

"Everything is possible. Don't you worry about this, Dr. Steele. You have plenty to worry about. Your metrics. The door-to-doc time. The patient complaints. Those are your responsibilities," Mike declared. "At this time, this does not appear to be an MD problem. As such, it's not your responsibility. I'll let you know if something changes."

He stood up. The conversation was over.

Mike was new. As ED director, he was responsible for the operations and the ED staff, all but the doctors. Emma, as medical director, was only in charge of the doctors. But issues were never isolated. They were complicated and multifactorial, involving everything and everybody. But Mike didn't want Emma's help. He needed to prove himself. Plus, Mike was a male nurse. Emma was a female doctor, bending the traditional gender roles where doctors were male, and nurses female. Mike chaffed.

Emma shrugged. *Technically, this isn't a doc problem. Not yet.*

"Let me know if you need my help."

She went to her patients, but deep inside she was weary. She knew something bad was going on. She just didn't know what.

21

Taylor woke up with a heavy heart. Then she remembered why. She had to call Eric.

She didn't want to. She'd rather not speak to Eric. But she didn't have a choice. Her mother would do as she promised. She always did.

She sighed and dialed his number.

"Taylor!"

"Yes."

"Where are you? I've been worried sick about you! How are you?"

"I'm OK."

"Where are you?"

She didn't want to tell him. She didn't want him coming to harass her. Though, once she told him... Maybe she could go with the rape story... No, that wouldn't fly. She'd just prove herself untrustworthy again.

"Let's meet."

"Where?"

"The library?"

"I'll be there in half an hour."

Taylor splashed cold water over her eyes to bring down the swelling. She put on mascara. Lots of it. She brushed her hair, for the first time in days. She put on dark sunglasses. She added a baseball cap, trying to hide.

Looking handsome but tired, Eric was waiting. His rapt smile made her heart ache. *This may be the end.*

He hugged her like he'd never let go.

"I missed you! What happened?"

Taylor sighed. She glanced around, looking for courage. No courage anywhere, just kids playing hopscotch on the sidewalk. Their smiling mothers, watching. Trees, sprouting fresh green leaves. Even the wind smelled moist and rich, heavy with the promise of growth, as it caressed her face.

The loss crushed her.

She had hoped to be like these parents. Loving, smiling, secretly proud that their kid was the best. The tallest, the smartest, the most successful.

That wasn't happening.

First, her kid was not their kid. Second, her kid was likely to be different. Between drinking and drugs, she had seen to that.

"Let's walk," she said, avoiding his eyes.

Hand in hand, they walked along the quiet street.

"Eric, I lied to you."

His hand gripped her tighter. She waited for the question, but it didn't come.

"I didn't really lie to you. I just omitted telling you some stuff."

"Like what?"

"I didn't tell you...I couldn't tell you...I...I just couldn't..."

Eric stopped. He took off her sunglasses. His luminous blue eyes melted her soul.

"It doesn't matter, Taylor. You don't need to tell me. The past is the past. I don't care. I love you."

Taylor's heart swelled. Then it shattered.

So much joy. So much pain.

She wanted to let it go. The past was the past.

But the past was not the past. The past was here. Growing into the future, right inside her. He'll notice, any day now. The past, the present, and the future, all here, right now. She had to deal with it.

"I wish it was so."

"It is. The past doesn't matter. What matters is now. What matters is the future. Our future."

She couldn't take it anymore.

"Eric, I'm pregnant."

His eyes lost focus. Then his face lit up.

Taylor understood. She didn't have to lie. He thought the baby was his. She could just let it go.

"That's wonderful! I..."

"It's not yours."

He frowned.

"The baby is not yours."

Scorched.

The light died. The ashes remained. Like the silent torment in Munch's scream, his face became a mask of pain.

He let go of her hand. His arms fell sideways like dead branches. His head hung.

"I'm sorry, Eric."

He nodded. Taylor felt as if she'd hit him.

"I'm sorry," she murmured.

"I see. I have to go now."

He left.

He didn't walk. He ran as if wolves were nipping at his heels. Taylor watched.

Her eyes followed him, hoping he'd stop, turn around, and come back. She could explain.

He didn't.

What do I do?

Her soul drowned in darkness. She felt empty inside. Painfully empty. Like a black hole.

She remembered the gun in her father's safe.

She knew the combination. She'd find a peaceful place. She wouldn't have to suffer any more. No more shame. No more pain. No more nightmares and sleepless nights, wondering if the baby was going to be normal or an abhorrent mistake of nature.

She wouldn't have to face her father, who had always loved and trusted her. She wouldn't have to see his disappointment.

She wouldn't have to face her mother either. She wouldn't say: "I told you so," but she didn't need to. If she'd listened, things would be better now. They could hardly be worse.

She made a beeline to her father's house. It was still early. Amber should be at work, the girls in school. There shouldn't be anyone home but the dogs. They won't ask questions.

She was right. Thelma and Louise jumped on her, yapping their love. She hugged them, scratched them and said good-bye.

The office was dark behind the heavy curtains. The safe combination hadn't changed. It was still her mother's birthday. She took the gun and the ammo. She put them in her pockets. She took a last look around. Nothing new but a frame on his desk. The picture of Amber with Opal and Iris had moved to the side. The new one was a snapshot of herself and her mother. Victor took it the day she went to rehab. She smiled, glowing with happiness, her dark hair ravaged by the wind. Emma, behind her, looked into the camera. Her coffee-colored eyes were smiling, tender and knowing. Her mother's eyes looked straight into her soul, as if she knew she was up to something. Again.

Taylor turned the picture face down and left.

Some parents are too much to bear.

"**M**ommy! Mommy!"

I look inside Room 14. She's crying, hugging a teddy bear.

She's not a kid. Not in forever. Her green eyes faded to white. Her skin is so thin it's transparent.

I step in.

"Are you my mother?"

"No." God forbid.

"Where's my mother?"

Her mother must be dead. She should be dead too, if the Almighty was kind. She's not.

"Can you call my mother?"

I check her ID. Ella. She's ninety.

"What do you need, Ella?"

She smiles.

"Can I have a cookie?"

"I'll get you a cookie."

By God's mercy, there are chocolate chip cookies in the break room.

"There you are, Ella."

"Thank you, Mommy. Where's my milk?"

Milk. I get her milk.

She gums the cookie. She chokes.

I take away her cookie.

"My cookie! My cookie!"

I check her chart. Dysphagia diet. Thickened fluids only.

She's screaming. I give back her cookie. She chokes again.

She's ninety, she wants her mother, and she can't even eat a cookie. She drops the cookie and starts screaming.

All right, Ella. How can I help you?

I'm running short on fentanyl. I don't have insulin handy. A pillow won't work for this one. She's too loud.

I spot the hypertonic saline on the counter. It's a concentrated salt solution that helps shrink swollen brains. They ordered it for the brain injury, but the patient that needed it is gone. Pharmacy's so slow, you'd think they made it from scratch.

I don't know if it works. And, if it does, it won't be fast. So what? What's the big rush? She's waited for ninety years!

I give her another cookie. I attach the hypertonic bag to her IV and squeeze it in as fast as I can.

My heart's pounding. I have no business being here. If they catch me, I'm toast. I'm not her nurse, Ben is. What if he comes in? I need to get out of here. I squeeze harder. I'm afraid I'll blow her IV.

The door opens. I hide the bag under the sheets and pretend I'm checking the IV.

It's X-ray. I smile.

"Come back in ten, please."

She leaves. I almost peed myself.

The bag's almost done. She's still gumming her cookie. This was iffy. Stupid too.

I wonder what will happen? Will her brain shrink? Or swell?

Shrink, I think. Maybe. It doesn't matter. I'm not doing that again.

I'll get some potassium pills. Crushed and injected, they should work.

It's not sterile. So what? They'll die before they get septic.

By the time her next shift came, Emma forgot about Mike and her uneasy feeling that something eerie was going on. She finished draining the swollen knee in Room 9. A full 30 cc syringe. The thick, straw-colored fluid was clear enough to read through. *Great. The knee's ugly, but the fluid looks good. It's not septic. Gout maybe?* She went back to her desk to find Alex waiting. As always, his thick round glasses enlarged his eyes, making him look puzzled.

"Can I run something by you?"

"Please."

"I had this nursing home patient yesterday. She had a urinary tract infection. She was a little confused, but she looked OK. I gave her fluids and antibiotics, and I sent her back."

"Yes."

"She's back today, and now she's completely altered. Her urine looks better, but her other labs are off. Yesterday her sodium was 135, her baseline. Today it's 160.

"Is she dehydrated?"

"Why should she be? She was fine yesterday. She's not vomiting, no diarrhea, she's drinking OK. Why would she be dehydrated?"

"Is she on Lasix?"

"They all are. They must put it in the water at the nursing home. But she's been on it forever."

"Anything else weird?"

"Nothing yet. I re-sent the labs to recheck."

"What are you thinking?"

"I'm wondering about a med error. What if somebody gave her hypertonic saline yesterday?"

"That's weird. Why would they? How could they? We don't even have that in the pixies. We have to order it from pharmacy. Who was her nurse?"

"Ben."

"Ben wouldn't make a mistake like that!"

"Of course not."

"What are you saying, Alex?"

"We've had strange things happening lately. A stable patient found dead. A non-diabetic with a glucose of 12. Now this. I'm wondering if there's a unifying explanation for all this."

Emma knew what he meant. She'd been wondering about that too. She couldn't believe it. But she couldn't ignore it, either.

"Give me her name. I'll look."

"Thanks. Let me know."

24

Halfway through her shift, Emma sat alone at the corner table in the cafeteria drinking tea. She was taking a rare break. She didn't want tea. She wanted wine. She wanted to go home. She needed sleep. But she still had hours to go, and she needed to speak to Victor.

The lunch hour hustle was long gone. Just a few scrubs reading segments of the same newspaper at different tables, looking lonely and bored. *I wish they served wine here. The staff would be happier. Patients and families too. French have wine with lunch and they are more productive than we are. Italians give their kids a splash of wine in their water as soon as they can drink from a glass. It removes the mystique. It makes it normal and ordinary, instead of hidden and attractive. That's why they have no binge drinking like we do. Never heard of college students dying from alcohol poisoning in Italy!*

She took another sip of tea, trying to ignore the conversation behind her. Out of all places, they had to talk right there. She recognized Carlos's soft Hispanic accent. The female was familiar too. Judy. She tried to hide, but she didn't need to. They were too busy to notice her.

"He sent that urine sample. Without gloves. Then stopped by the break room and dug into the pizza, without washing his hands."

"Really?" Carlos said. "Disgusting. What a piece of shit."

"Be careful, Carlos. He has a lot of friends."

"I don't care."

"Hi, Emma." Victor hugged her and kissed her cheek. With his curly gray hair covering his ears, his John Lennon glasses magnifying his eyes, and his jeans instead of a suit, he looked like an aging hippie rather than a cardiologist. He sat, smiled, and took her hand in his.

"What's up, Em? I hope it's not bad news."

"Nope. Taylor is back." Emma took back her hand and rested it on her knee.

Victor sighed. His shoulders softened.

"Thank God. Where is she? What happened?"

"She left the rehab and hitchhiked home."

"Why?"

"How much time do you have?"

"Not much. I've got the pager."

"Eric proposed to her."

"Proposed to her? She's only seventeen."

"For another month or so."

"Still, she's far too young..."

Emma shrugged. "Either way. He proposed to her. She took off because she had lied to him. She didn't tell him."

"Tell him what?"

"Well...she's pregnant."

"Again?"

"Still."

"Still?"

"Yep. That day she went for an abortion, she didn't get one. She changed her mind. Then, when they started dating, she didn't tell him she was pregnant. Now that she started showing, she had to tell him. She ran away instead."

Victor sighed. "Is she OK?"

"She looks OK. She doesn't want to see a doctor."

Victor smiled.

"I mean an OBGYN. I'm not her doctor, I'm her mother!"

"You're still a doctor."

"Well, you know how we ER folks are about family…"

"I do. Remember when you sent her to school for a week before you got an X-ray to find her broken wrist?"

"It was just a buckle fracture. There was nothing to do about it anyhow."

Victor laughed. "That's so you!"

"That's so ER."

"Is she OK?"

"Not bad. She's upset. She didn't call Eric. I told her that if she didn't, I would."

"Have you called him?"

"Not yet."

"Emma, let her be. Give her time."

"I did. She's been back for three days."

"Yes, but…"

"No but. She needs to grow up. She is responsible for her relationships. She needs to get straight with him. He deserves that."

"But Emma, she's just a kid…"

"She's about to be a mother. She needs to grow up. Fast."

"You're always so hard on her!"

"And you're always so soft! No wonder she's spoiled rotten!"

"She's your kid, Emma! Be kind!"

"You're kind enough for both of us! Someone needs to hold her responsible!"

"I guess you're right. I am too soft with her." Victor took off his glasses and started wiping them with the bottom of his shirt, like he always did when he was thinking. "Now what?"

"It's up to her."

"I'll stop by to see her later. Or tomorrow. No, not tomorrow. Amber's going out with her friends. I need to get home early to watch the kids."

Emma smiled. Ten years ago, it had been heartbreaking seeing Amber take her place. Now it was fun to watch.

Victor cleared his voice. "You know, Emma... I..."

Trouble in paradise?

"I miss you."

What?

"I never thought things would turn out like they did. I missed you as soon as I left. I still do. I wish I didn't do what I did, ten years ago. I wish things were different."

What are you saying?

"I never loved anybody the way I loved you."

Yep. That's what you're saying. Seriously? Has Amber dropped you? Or you've gotten tired of working your ass off to pay the bills?

"I wish we could go back," he said, his voice almost a whisper.

Oh no, we're not going there. Never again. Emma smiled her best smile.

"Wouldn't that be nice? But we can't. Life is what it is. Going back is not an option. Don't worry about me, I'm OK. And you have Amber. You have your two beautiful girls. And Thelma and Louise. You have a full, beautiful life."

Victor's blue eyes embraced her.

"I'm not worried about you..."

"Great. I have to go now." Emma stood.

Victor caught her hand. "Emma, I..."

His pager rang.

Thank God!

"Bye, Victor. I'll tell Taylor you're coming."

She took off so fast that the napkins followed in her wake, and she didn't look back.

I'll be damned!

25

Taylor didn't know where to go. She walked and walked. Her right hand, in her pocket, held the gun. She looked for the place. A good place. A quiet place.

No such place downtown. Everybody was out, having a good time. Everybody but her.

She walked, her shoulders carrying her life burden. She didn't care for the breeze caressing her face. She didn't feel the sun warming her. She didn't even need to pee.

She only felt the rough, firm grip of the gun. The gun, heavier than the ammunition in her left pocket, unbalanced her gait, but she didn't notice. She was too busy looking for a good place to die.

She left the town behind. The forest started. The old pines shielded her in silence. Incense-like resin cleansed the air. Her feet sunk into the soft carpet of pine needles. The quietude embraced her. No birds, no flowers, no grass. Just peace. And dusky green light, one hour before sunset.

This was it. She walked into it like she'd walk into her shroud. She looked for the right spot. She found it. A fallen tree covered in moss, surrounded by saplings. She stopped to listen to the silence.

Inside her head, the voices started.

"I've never loved anybody like I love you. Nothing you can do will make me love you less."

"You need to tell him. He may leave. Or not. You must tell him. He'll find out anyhow. He'll leave. Not because of the baby. Because of the lie."

"You're my lovely little angel. You can do no wrong."

"Maybe if I wait, he's going to love me enough to not care that I'm pregnant."

"You can't build your life on a lie. You need to tell him!"

The voices taunted her. Lied to her. Tortured her.

She took out the gun and set it on the trunk. She loaded it carefully, like her father had taught her. They used to shoot together, just the two of them. Before Amber came. Then Iris. Then Opal.

She rolled her jacket and made it into a pillow. She laid the loaded gun on her chest and rested her hands on the moss-covered bark. She thought about her good days. Not many. Shooting with her father. Laughing with Eric. Her mother dropping her at the rehab.

Father will miss me. But he's got Opal and Iris to love instead. And Amber. Funny, I've never been jealous of Amber like I am of Mother. I've always felt the need to compete with Mother. That's a nonstarter. She's always right. She knows everything. She sees through people.

Taylor didn't like that. Inside her, it wasn't pretty. She was selfish and manipulative. She would do anything to have her way. Nobody knew it. Not Father, nor Eric, not even her, most of the time. Nobody but her mother. *We don't love people who make us feel small.*

Eric said he'd love her no matter what. He abandoned her, only minutes later. He'd be sorry.

She envisioned her funeral. *Mother, dressed in black, her eyes dry. Father, crying, wiping his glasses with his shirt. Eric, sobbing and throwing himself over the casket, covering my hands with kisses. I'll be cold and beautiful in my blue dress. Like a Madonna. They'll be sorry.*

But will Mother know which dress? And how to do my hair? She wished she'd left instructions. She took out her cell phone and started an email. "Blue dress. Mascara. Sapphire earrings. Peacock feathers bag."

She sent it to herself, knowing they'd find it. She laid back. The moss was moist and soft, vegetal velvet smelling like the forest. She listened to a rustle in the branches, wondering what it was. *What if something eats me before they find me? What if there's no cold white hand for Eric to cry on, and no eyelashes for mascara? Even ears for the earrings?*

She shuddered and sat up. *There are no wild animals here. But what if I rot before they find me? What if the birds eat my eyes?* A wave of nausea. She bent over to retch. She took a deep breath, then another. *Who cares? I'll be dead. I won't see it anyhow. So what if they do a closed casket? Eric can cry over my picture. I bet he will.*

She rearranged her jacket and lay back. She took a few cleansing breaths. She picked up the gun. She placed the barrel against her right temple. It was cold.

It's going to blow up my face. There'll be no Madonna to look at.

She thought about putting the barrel in her mouth, to blow off the back of her head instead. That wouldn't show as she laid on her back in the casket. The smell of the gun made her nauseous. *There's nothing like puking as you try to shoot yourself.*

She moved the gun to her heart. The angle was awkward. Her wrist wouldn't flex that far. She'd have to pull the trigger with her thumb. She found the space between her second and third left ribs. She sat the barrel right there, perpendicular to the chest. Her right hand shook. She steadied it with her left. She took a deep breath.

Something moved. She froze. It moved again.

Deep inside her, the baby was moving. *I can't believe it.*

She put down the gun and cupped her swollen belly with her palms. Like a butterfly fluttering his wings, he waved again.

"I'm here, remember?"

She choked. She covered her face with her hands and cried. She cried until she ran out of tears.

She unloaded the gun. She put it in her pocket and headed home. She was somebody's home. She had no right to die.

26

---

isgusting. He called me disgusting. Me!

That piece of shit impotent jerk called me disgusting.

I want to crush him. I want to break his neck. I want to set him on fire. I want to destroy him.

How?

Killing him would be easy. But it doesn't hurt enough.

I'll make him lose what matters most to him. I'll destroy him little by little. I'll take away everything he's built. He'll be sorry he was ever born. His friends will despise him and his parents will wish they never fucked.

Better than breaking his neck. I'll break his spirit.

They say revenge is better served cold. I'll start cooking.

You'll be sorry you were ever born, motherfucker!

Where do I start?

Then it comes to me.

Life is good.

Death is better.

27

Her shift almost over, Emma finished examining the back pain in Room 5. Her back was hurting too. She looked forward to going home to lie down and think through the events of her day, from her talk with Alex to the funny meeting with Victor.

The patient looked fine. Good strength, no numbness, no red flags. *It's just a strained back. What is it with these people that they can't resist moving refrigerators?*

She put in orders and told Carlos, "Let's give the guy in Room 5 some Toradol and Valium. I wrote for some morphine too, but please don't give it with the Valium. He may never wake up."

Carlos grumbled.

Emma shrugged. *He's mad that I told him something he already knows. Too bad. It's better than killing somebody.* She went back to running the board. There was a new chest pain in Room 4. Emma went to see her.

The room was a screaming cacophony of alarms. Monitors beeped at a pulse of 160. The blood pressure was low. Gray and shriveled, her eyes closed, the woman gasped for air. By her side, a man held her hand, his eyes wide with fright.

She's fixing to die.

"I need a nurse. Now," Emma called.

Carlos rushed in.

"Let's move her to a front room. IV. Pacer. EKG. The whole nine yards."

The scrubs poured in. They pushed the stretcher down the hallway to Room 2. Carlos stuck on the pacer pads, front and back. Judy looked for IV access. Amy struggled to make the monitor leads stick to the skin, but they wouldn't. The skin was slick with sweat.

She's diaphoretic. Her heart is way too fast. And irregular. She's in atrial fibrillation. The blood pressure's soft. She looks like crap. I'm afraid to give her anything and drop her blood pressure even more. We may need to shock her out of it, and that rarely works in A-fib.

"What do we have for IV access?" Emma asked.

"I got an 18 in," Judy said. "I'm working on a second."

"You're a champ. Let's start fluids."

Emma listened to the lungs, making sure they weren't already drowning. "I need an old EKG. And a cardiologist."

"EKG coming," Amy said.

"Blood pressure?"

"It's too low to measure. I'm getting a manual. 68/42."

Crap.

"Get ready to cardiovert. Get Sal. We need push pressors." *They should increase her blood pressure enough to let me use some drugs.*

Sal materialized as if she'd summoned him.

"Push pressors."

"Which one?"

"Phenylephrine. That should increase her blood pressure without messing up the pulse even more."

Sal produced a 10cc syringe out of his pocket. "How much?"

"2 cc every three to five minutes."

"The code cart's here," Carlos said. "You want to intubate?"

"I can't. I'd drop her blood pressure. That would kill her. I have to wait. Let's try 25 of fentanyl."

"Twenty-five of fentanyl given," Judy said.

That's abysmal, but it will help a little with the pain. I don't have enough pressure to sedate her.

"Let's try 100 volts."

Carlos charged the defibrillator. "All clear?"

They stepped back. He pushed the button.

The current went from pad to pad, across the skin, through the chest to get to the heart and shock it out of its crazy rhythm. The power of the current lifted her off the stretcher. She screamed. She fell back.

The rhythm didn't change.

I hate A-fib. Nasty, stubborn SOB. At least the pressors helped the blood pressure. A little.

"Let's do another 25 of fentanyl. Charge at 150 this time." *What the heck? Why cook her slowly? May as well do the best we can, right now. While she's still alive.*

"Let's do 200."

Carlos moved the button to 200.

"Everybody clear?"

The scream splintered the air. The woman levitated above the stretcher, then fell back, limp.

Silence. The heart had stopped.

Emma stared at the monitor. She waited a few seconds.

Nothing. *The monitor line's flat as a pancake. She's in asystole. Damn!*

"Start CPR."

Carlos took a deep breath and clasped his hands together to start CPR. He leaned over the stretcher, just as the monitor beeped again. The heart restarted at 120 beats per minute.

That was close. "Blood pressure?"

"95/60."

Joy flooded the room. They breathed. They celebrated. They had saved her.

Emma smiled and touched the old man's shoulder. "She's OK."

Slow tears ran down his sunbaked wrinkles. He touched her hand.

Emma took it. She hugged him. She held him tight to give him strength.

"Good work, team."

They smiled. That's what they lived for.

Emma went back to her desk to check the board. An eerie feeling fluttered inside her, chasing away the joy. Something, somewhere, was wrong.

The back pain in Room 5? She went to check on him.

He was no longer hurting.

28

I t was almost tomorrow by the time Carlos got home. The death of Room 5 produced a shitstorm like nothing he'd seen before. They interviewed him for hours, asking him countless stupid questions. All of them. Mike, Risk Management, the lawyer, some other suits he didn't even know.

None of them ever touched a patient. They didn't know what it was like to live in the trenches. To wear shit-stained scrubs. To wonder if you'd make it to the bathroom. To get abused every single shift. The suits inhabited a different world.

He parked his Subaru behind George's Ford and rested his forehead on the steering wheel. George was home. He could use a drink and a friend. But the lawyer had warned him: "Keep mum. No talking. Anything you say can be used against you. All communications, except those with your lawyer, are discoverable."

This death was likely to go to court. His patient, a healthy man, had died for no reason. They had worked on him for an hour. Nothing helped. Nobody understood what happened.

"Heart attack? Stroke? Dissection?" Dr. Greene asked.

"I don't know," Dr. Steele said. "Nothing makes any sense. He was fine an hour ago. His back pain was purely mechanical. He had strained his back, moving furniture. Unless I'm wrong. I hope the autopsy helps us understand."

Dr. Usher was passing by. She laughed.

"That's how you diagnose your patients, Emma? Via autopsy? What's wrong with a good old CT scan? If you figure it out before they die, you may even save them, you know?"

Dr. Steele smiled. Not a nice smile. Carlos hoped she'd never smile at him like that. Like a barn cat seeing a mouse on crutches.

"Thanks, Ann. I'll keep that in mind. Carlos, when did you see him last?"

"Before you called me for the arrhythmia. I was about to give him the meds you ordered."

"Did you give them?"

"No. But I got them out of the locked med room."

"Where are they?"

"I left them on the desk, but they're gone. Maybe some-body gave them as we worked on the A-fib patient?"

"What does the computer say?" Dr. Steele asked.

The computer said nothing. Nurses helped each other with meds, IVs, or labs, when it got busy. But this time nobody had offered to help.

"We'll have a root case analysis," Mike said. "We'll find out who's responsible."

Somebody was going to face the music. Either Dr. Steele for missing the diagnosis, or him, for losing track of the meds. Carlos hoped it wasn't him.

He sighed, got out of his truck, and opened the door. George was in the living room, watching a game.

"Grab a beer and come here," he shouted.

Grateful, Carlos grabbed a Bud Light, George's go-to beer: "It's good for the kidneys. Keeps them afloat. Good exercise too. Every ten minutes, it gets you off the sofa to the bathroom."

Carlos sat in Mary's old rocking chair. He took a swig. *Piss-like. But cold.*

George glanced at him. "Bad day?"

"Yeah."

"Want to talk about it?"

"I can't."

"Legal?"

"Yeah."

"Want to talk about the game then?"

Carlos sighed. George was a decent man and a good friend. He'd taken him in without asking questions. He never pried. He was always there.

"I don't know much about the game," Carlos said, looking at the score of well-fed men stumbling over each other.

"Neither do they. It's not worth watching, but it's company."

"You must be lonely since Mary died."

"Yep. She was my high-school sweetheart. I've never cared about another woman. I never will."

"You're lucky."

"I guess I am. You?"

Carlos shrugged "I found out that Faith was seeing someone else. She had us move here so she could be with him. Now it's too late to go back."

"Is she still with him?"

"No."

"If she dragged you here, she cared about you. Maybe she still does. Did you speak to her?"

"I'm not interested."

"Why not? If you love her..."

"I can't."

He remembered the morning after. Faith approached him at work. She took his hand. He pulled away.

"Don't touch me."

"Why not? That's not what you said last night..."

"You make me sick."

Faith paled. Her indigo blue eyes swallowed her face, making her look like an alien. "Really!"

"Really. Don't ever touch me again."

She smiled.

"You might change your mind."

"Never."

"Never is a long time."

"Not long enough."

He left. Her eyes burned his back like embers. He shivered and took another sip of beer.

"Never again."

29

Taylor walked back home from the forest. It took hours. Her feet hurt and her throat was scorched with thirst, but her baby was alive. She laid down in her bed, thinking about Eric and the things she should have told him. She waited for the baby to move again.

The doorbell rang. She ignored it.

It rang again. Taylor pulled the pillow over her head.

Her phone vibrated. She huffed. *What's wrong with people? Why can't they leave me alone?*

But what if it's Eric? Calling to tell me that I'm still the love of his life?!"

She threw the pillow and grabbed her phone. *Dad.*

She loved him, but she wanted nothing to do with him right now. She went back to bed.

The doorbell rang again.

What if it's Eric at the door?

She went to the mirror. Her swollen eyes looked like overripe plums, her hair like a snake nest. *I can't see him like this! But what if he leaves? I won't even know if it's him!* She splashed cold water over her face and rubbed her skin till it burned. She looked in the mirror again. Her burning cheeks made her eyes look OK. She opened the door.

It was her father. It was April and mellow, but he looked like a man in a snowstorm. His eyes were no better than hers: wet, muddled, sorrowful. He sobbed. He pressed her to his heart. He let go. He held her at arms' length, looking her up and down.

"Where is it?"

"Where is what?"

"My gun. You took it. Where is it?"

"How do you know it was me? Maybe..."

"Cut the crap, Taylor. You're the only one who knows the code. If I had any sense, I'd have changed it last time. You were gone, so I thought it was safe. I was wrong, and I was lazy. Where is it?"

Taylor shrugged. "What do you need it for?"

"I don't. I need you not to have it. Where is it? Who were you going to shoot this time?"

Taylor felt hurt. *It's not like I walk around shooting people on a regular basis. I never shot anyone yet. The one time I was close, I had good reasons. Just like Father to overreact!*

"It's in my room."

Secretly, she was relieved. She had been close. She didn't want to go back. She couldn't afford to. She had a responsibility. She had to go on until her baby was born. Afterwards, she could give it up for adoption. Or she could bring it up on her own. She had hoped it was going to be with Eric. No more. Either way, she was going to stay alive long enough to give the kid a chance to live. *Five more months. After that, I'm free. Mother will do her best for the kid, if I'm not here.*

Victor headed toward her room like he still lived there. He went straight to the wardrobe and opened the lowest left drawer. He pushed the button unlocking the secret compartment and grabbed the gun and the ammo. He removed the magazine, checked there was no bullet in the chamber, and stuffed everything in his pockets.

He went back to the living room and sat in his old green armchair. He took off his round glasses and wiped them with the bottom of his shirt. He put them back and looked her in the eye.

"What's this about?"

This wasn't her father. Her father was always kind and patient. He never blamed her for anything. When she messed up, he hugged her, telling her she'd do better next time. *Now this.*

"What do you mean?"

"You know damn well what I mean. Why did you elope? Why didn't you tell me? And why did you steal my gun?"

His words held no softness. He was straight and matter-of-fact. Like her mother, for fuck's sake! She looked in his eyes, forcing out a tear.

He frowned. "Get to it, Taylor! I'm on call. My beeper's about to go off. Unless I'm sure you're safe, I can't leave you alone. I'll have to call 911. I'll tell them that you stole my gun and you're suicidal. They'll come and they'll take you to the ER. Your mother may or may not be working. I don't know which is worse. Get to it, and get to it now!"

This side of him she'd never seen. She told him about the failed abortion. About Eric. About her mother's advice. She told him that Eric ditched her. She told him how she wanted to end her life but couldn't.

He listened.

"You love Eric?"

She sobbed.

"Are you sure?"

She came undone over that one. She cried and cried. He

held her to comfort her. His hold was love and safety. But it wasn't Eric.

"Listen, Taylor. I'll tell you something you can never tell anyone."

Taylor nodded.

"If you do, a lot of people will get hurt. Including me."

"OK."

"I still love your mother."

Taylor's jaw fell. *Are you kidding?*

He wasn't.

"Ten years ago, I was infatuated with Amber. She was young, pretty, submissive. She was everything your mother wasn't. We had an affair. She got pregnant. I thought I was being honorable when I left you and your mother to marry Amber. We had Opal. Then Iris. I never worried about you. I knew your mother was going to look after you. I loved you, I wanted you to be happy, but I never worried about you."

Taylor nodded.

"I never worried about your mother either. She's the strongest person I know. She survived Vincent's death alone. She didn't need me. That's hard to take, for a man who wants to be a man. She was who she was. I was who I was. We broke apart."

Taylor nodded.

"It took me a couple of years to realize that I didn't really love Amber. She was pretty. Men envied me. But she wasn't your mother. Nobody is like your mother."

That, Taylor knew.

He took off his glasses and started wiping them again.

"Your mother..."

The beeper went off.

"I need to go."

He hugged her.

"I love you. I'm glad you're alive. I'll change the code on that damn safe. Maybe even get rid of the damn gun.""

"Father..."

"Yes?" He climbed in his old Subaru.

"What are you saying?"

"I'm saying that there is no end to love. If Eric loves you, he'll be back. If you love him, you'll take him back. I'd take your mother back in a heartbeat."

"Would she?"

"She won't, baby. She's smarter than that."

Taylor had never thought about her mother as an object of love. *She's old and always tired. Her hair's a mess. And her clothes! And still, she's attractive and desirable. Or so Father thinks.*

More than Amber.

Really?

30

H ours after her shift, Emma was still in her office. Her back hurt and her stomach grumbled as she combed through chart after chart. Something bad was happening. Her patients were dying. She had to figure out what it was and stop it. She didn't care what Mike, Gus, or the Risk Management people had to say. This last death, her back pain patient, forced her to get involved. No matter what, she had to stop the deaths.

Her stomach burned with hunger. *Another half hour.* She took another sip of water, pulled her jacket closer, and returned to her charts.

Four cases. What did they have in common?

The first one was the rash. Kurt's patient. She combed through the EMR. Vitals. Triage note. Nurse's note. Repeat vitals. Orders. There was nothing wrong. The glucose was fine. No insulin order.

Still, she died. Her last glucose was abysmal. Somehow, she got insulin. But how? Insulin is locked in the med room. You need the code, then two IDs: one for the patient, one for the nurse. It's a tight system. Nobody but nurses and pharmacists can remove meds.

But insulin is easy to get. Many have it at home. Including Carlos. And George, his roommate.

Kurt had ordered insulin for the patient next door. What happened to it? She went through chart after chart looking for a hyperglycemic male in Room 21. She found him. Bob Sexton. Blood glucose 550. Normal is 100. An order for 30 units of insulin. His glucose was unchanged an hour later.

She had to speak to Sal to find out who gave it. She took a screen shot, though she knew she was violating HIPPA. *If they catch me, I'm toast. People got fired for less. So? I'm the medical director. Patient safety is my responsibility, no matter what Mike says.*

She looked for the second case. *Oops! This was the second case! The first case was Alex's hip fracture.* Finding the chart was easy. The only hip fracture who died that day. She combed through it. She found the autopsy report. *Broken hip, arteriosclerosis, aging brain, yada yada. The tox report isn't back.*

The vitals bothered her. The initial pulse and blood pressure were high. Then, the last set of vitals were normal. *It looks like she's getting better, then, half an hour later, she's dead. Why?*

She took another snapshot. She started a list.

This is patient #1.

Patient #2 is the hypoglycemia.

Patient #3 is Alex's dehydration with altered mental status. She didn't die, but she was close. The chart looked fine.

Patient # 4 is my back pain. Normal vitals. No labs, no radiology. The autopsy will take a while. This one was neither old nor sick. Just a run-of-the-mill back pain. Carlos said he left the drugs on the counter. They disappeared. Where? Did somebody give them? Did I miss some pathology that killed him? A dissection? An aneurysm?

She went back looking for similarities.

Three different doctors: Alex in the first case, Kurt in the second, Alex again in the third. The last case was hers.

Three nurses: Brenda. Carlos. Ben. Carlos again.

Four patients: #1: Female, 86, nursing home. #2: Female, 88, married. #3: Female, 90, nursing home. #4: male, 50s, healthy.

That back pain doesn't fit. Is there a pattern? Or just bad luck? A string of unrelated things? People die in the ER all the time. They come because they think they're dying. They're often right.

Her stomach grumbled again, loud enough to hear it from the parking lot. The water bottle was empty. It was late. She had another shift tomorrow. Taylor was home alone.

She grabbed her bag and headed home, leaving the door unlocked for the cleaning crew.

That was perfect. I couldn't do any better. Too bad he had to die. Well, at least he's no longer drug-seeking.

Poor Emma. She wonders if she missed something. I wish I could tell her.

Getting away from the pattern was good. It keeps them on their toes.

Did you like that, Carlos, you stupid spic? You shouldn't leave your meds on the counter! I had to give him a little extra, of course. There wasn't enough there to kill him.

As I head out to lunch, I see the guy in Room 3. He's on a bipap mask. The ventilator's breathing for him as he sleeps. He's Carlos's patient. I take his mask off.

Actually, I can do better. I put the mask back on his face but I detach it from the vent.

I watch the oxygen saturation plummet. 90. 85. 79.

He's turning a nice shade of purple.

74.

I'd better leave before they find me here.

68.

32

As she came in for her evening shift, Emma found Faith playing with the baby in Room 4. She smiled. Beautiful and vibrant in her ironed green scrubs, Faith looked like a light had turned on inside her. No more sadness, misery, and tears. Happy Faith was back.

"How are you, Faith?"

"I'm great, Dr. Steele. You?"

"Good. Thanks again for the other day. I wouldn't be here if it wasn't for you."

"Yes, you would. I took you on that mountaintop. The least I could do was to get you back."

Emma laughed. "If you put it that way..."

"Are you...are you up to doing something again?"

"Absolutely. If you'll keep an eye on me."

"I always do, Dr. Steele! You're my hero!"

Emma blushed.

"Just tell me when and where." *I can use the exercise. And a friend.*

"Dr. Steele to Room 1."

The patient in Room 1 wasn't having a good day. Neither

were Judy and Suzy, trying to get her from the wheelchair to the stretcher. Her purple left foot hung by the skin. She wailed as they tried to move her. Emma went to help. She bent over to hold the foot as Judy and Suzy grabbed her arms. On a count of three, they got her on the stretcher. The foot flipped sideways, flat on the bed. The woman hollered in agony.

Emma cupped the heel, pulling the foot away towards its normal position. She held it there.

"Splinting materials. An IV. Morphine. Ortho."

Judy took off.

"A chair for the gentleman."

The man holding on to the sink was white as a sheet. Suzy pushed a chair under him and he crumbled.

Emma watched as she held on to the foot, maintaining its proper alignment. The sobs faded. The foot faded too, first to white, then to pink. The blood flow was back.

"I'm sorry about this. Your ankle's broken. I had to reposition it to restore its blood flow. We'll give you something for pain."

"It already feels better."

"What happened?"

"My horse spooked. I fell off and he stepped on my ankle."

Emma cringed. "Does anything else hurt?"

"No. That's it."

That ankle's shot. The orthopod won't like it.

He didn't. He treated her like she was a moron, as usual, but he took the patient to the OR. Emma went back to her desk to find Alex waiting.

"You have a minute?"

"Of course," she lied, looking at the full board.

He glanced around. People, everywhere. Room 5 was empty. They went in and closed the door.

"Emma, something's happening in our ER. Have you heard about my case, yesterday?"

"Not yet."

"A demented nursing home patient. Old smoker, short of breath, oxygen dependent. I threw the kitchen sink at him: breathing treatments, steroids, antibiotics. Magnesium. Bipap. He's fighting it, but he's improving. I go see another patient. I come back. He's blue. I had to intubate."

"That happens. They're confused. They don't like the mask. They pull it off. Then Bam! Their oxygen's down, their CO_2 is up, and they're altered."

"He wasn't that bad. He wasn't even blue! And he was improving. What's worse, though, his mask wasn't pulled off. It was detached from the vent."

"That's weird."

"Did you notice that people are dying like flies here? All old and demented."

"Except for my back pain."

"Yes...that one doesn't fit. But all the others..."

"Alex, they are sick. They're old. Their prognosis is bad to start with. Some die!"

Alex rolled his eyes. "Emma, you know better..."

"But there's been a lot of weird stuff. Are you thinking what I'm thinking?"

Alex nodded. "I think we have a mercy killer."

"What about the back pain? Where's the mercy in that?"

Alex shrugged. "That one is an outlier. Maybe it's not in this string."

"Or maybe it's the key. One death that is not like the others. Why?"

Alex shrugged.

"I saw this movie. The killer murdered a bunch of people just to cover the one crime he intended."

"What if it's the other way around? What if the back pain is the only one he didn't mean to kill?"

"Why kill him, then?"

"Exactly. Why kill him? That may be the answer we're looking for."

33

Emma's shift ended at midnight. The hospital appeared empty as she walked out through the quiet hallways. Her car sat alone in the dark parking lot. Emma remembered February's bloodbath and she shivered. *That debacle is over. Get over it.*

What if I called Zagarian?

They hadn't spoken in weeks. Ever since she blocked his calls.

But now when she needed somebody to run things by, Zagarian was it. He was smart, funny, and good-looking. He was a detective and he knew how to keep his mouth shut.

Except that she didn't want to speak to him. She didn't want to see him either.

They had dated for a few weeks. Sort of. They ate, drank, and laughed together. And at each other. It was fun. Until he wanted more.

Emma's sex life was as extinct as the dinosaurs. There had been a couple of men after Victor. None worth remembering. Then, as she got older, Taylor grew into a full-time job. She consumed all the time and energy Emma had left after work, so she stopped dating.

She didn't miss it. Not that much. *Sex is overrated. Wine is better, and it doesn't judge you.*

She was busy. So busy, that taking care of herself fell by the wayside. She gained weight. She was uncomfortable getting naked.

It didn't matter, as long as she was strong enough to relocate hips, intubate obese people, and run around the department without getting out of breath. Summer was short in the North Country. Parkas got way more use than bathing suits. Her social life was nil. So, who cared?

Zagarian did. That night he drove her home, he came in for a nightcap. She couldn't say no. They drank Grand Marnier and watched the fire. They talked about art, travel, and wine. They laughed.

He got close. He touched her cheek. He caressed her neck. Warmth spread throughout her body, awakening it. Her heart pounded. Her insides tingled.

His hand slid to her breast. She panicked. She jumped off the sofa, pretending to feed the fire. She didn't go back. The conversation died.

He waited. She couldn't think of anything to say.

"Why, Emma?"

"I...I work tomorrow. I need to sleep. I'm sorry."

He nodded and saw himself out.

She spent the night twisting and turning.

Why?

Because I'm fat. I'm embarrassed to be naked. I don't want anyone to see my rolls, my wrinkles, my legs. I don't want anyone to see me.

That was true. She didn't want him to see her. But there was more. She wasn't good enough. She wasn't worthy. Her mother taught her early that nobody would ever love her for herself. They'd love what she had to offer: money, comfort, status, sex. Then they'd get rid of her. Victor and Taylor proved it.

I'm not worth loving.

She couldn't handle any more rejection. She was fine by herself. She did her best as a doctor, as a mother, as a human, to maintain her self-respect. Love? She didn't need it. She couldn't open herself and be vulnerable. And get hurt again. *It's not worth it.*

She hadn't seen Zagarian after that night. He emailed. She didn't answer. He called. She didn't return his calls. He came to see her at work. She escaped through the ambulance door.

He stopped calling. But now...she had a problem. She needed help. This was professional, not personal. Maybe they could go back to their professional relationship. To being friends, without the physical stuff she didn't want to think about.

She called him.

"Please leave a message."

She hung up.

That evening, she opened one of her better wines. Stratus, a rich, smooth Canadian Red from Niagara on the Lake. Ripe with dark cherry and berry, generous, voluptuous, and smooth. It gave her solace and made her warm inside.

Not as warm as Zagarian.

Warm enough.

T hat was close. I went back to Room 3 to reconnect the vent, so they wouldn't notice. But they were already in there. I pretended I came to help with the intubation.

Carlos stared.

Careful, Angel. You're making mistakes.

You have all the time in the world!

The slower you cook him, the more he'll hurt!

Take it easy!

35

Sitting behind the flimsy curtain in Room 12.1, Carlos was having trouble getting blood. He had tried twice already with no luck. The woman had lived a rough life. Thanks to a long love affair with drugs, her veins were shot. *Track marks everywhere. An egg-sized abscess by her left elbow. That must be a recent injection. She looks ill. She'll need the whole nine yards. Thank God that her blood pressure's OK. For now.*

The woman shivered, gathering the flimsy cotton blanket around her.

"How are you feeling?"

"Like crap," she answered, her teeth chattering.

Carlos looked again for IV access. *I could get a tiny twenty-two in her thumb, but that won't be enough. I need a bigger vein, but she's mangled them all.*

A stretcher clanged behind the curtain to Room 12.2.

An old voice. Shaky. "What are you doing? Stop it! Stop it! I'll tell Mother."

"It's all right," Faith said, her voice soft as velvet. "We'll take care of you, Edna. Just relax."

"Mother? Is that you?"

"You're OK. I just need to check your blood pressure."

"She won't let you get blood," another voice said.

Ben.

"Mother, are you my mother?"

"You're OK, Edna. I'll take care of you. We just need to get some blood. A tiny prick..."

"Mother, where were you? They were mean to me."

"I'm sorry, Edna. Please let go of my hand."

Her soft voice warmed Carlos's heart. He took his time looking for that vein.

"Hold her hand. I'll get the IV," Ben said.

"Thanks, Ben. Just a little prick, OK, Edna?"

"Yes, Mother."

"What a good girl."

"Aaargh!"

"All done. Relax. It's over. Would you like some juice?"

"Grape?"

"You got it. Thanks, Ben."

"No problem. I'm always glad to help you."

"Thanks."

"Faith...I have two tickets for the Mellowship. On Friday. Would you like to come?"

"I...have to check my schedule."

"At seven. A cover for The Avengers. We could have dinner on the way."

"That would be nice."

"Great. I'll pick you up at four."

"I live in the..."

"I know where you live."

"Really? How come?"

"I know a lot of things about you, Faith." He laughed a low, dirty laugh.

"Like what?"

"I've been watching you…"

"Really? And?"

"I'll tell you on Friday."

Hands shaking, Carlos blew through the vein.

His patient screamed.

"Sorry," Carlos mumbled, low enough to not be heard next door.

He sat, holding pressure on the vein he'd blown.

"There's your grape juice, Edna."

"Thanks, Mommy. Can I have a cookie?"

36

The modern new gym was all blinding lights and mirrors. No place to hide. Emma stopped to catch her breath. She wiped the sweat off her face with her towel and sat on a weight bench, watching Faith give the instructor a run for his money. Faith had invited her to try an MMA class. Emma thought that would be fun. Now she knew better.

Thankfully, it was just them and the instructor. Emma didn't need any more audience. She looked like a fighting hippopotamus. She'd sprained her hip. She was spent. Now, past trying to keep up, she struggled to keep breathing. Fortunately the instructor, a handsome brown man moving like a hungry tiger, was nice to her and pretended not to notice she had stopped..

Emma had been kickboxing in her basement for months. both for exercise and self-defense, and she thought she was doing all right. But this class was something else. It kicked her butt. Not Faith's, though. Faith was a natural. Her feet kicking above her head, her strong body glowing with sweat, she smiled with delight. Emma was glad she wasn't her opponent.

Waiting for Faith to be done, she read the orange poster with the MMA rules. She liked "Rule #8: No fingers in the opponent's orifices." Putting fingers in orifices—she did that for a living. It wasn't that much fun.

After the class, they strolled along the river, enjoying the afternoon sun. They sat on a bench, sipping ice tea, watching the mesmerizing Hudson River heading home, and listening to the birds chirping in secret codes.

"You're good! You're sure you haven't done this before?" Emma asked.

Faith laughed. "Not this. But I did other things. Everything you try teaches you something. Life is learning."

After all she's been through, she's still optimistic and full of joy. I wish it was contagious!

"How are you doing, Faith?"

"I'm doing great. Ben just asked me out."

"Really?" *Last time we met, she was heartbroken about Carlos. That was what? Last week?*

"Ben? Our Ben?"

"Yes. He invited me to a concert."

"But...I thought he was married?"

"Yes, but they don't get along. They've been talking about separation."

"But didn't they recently have twins?

"A few months ago."

"You think it's a good idea to date him?"

"I'm not serious about him. I don't think he's serious about me either. He asked me out just to spite Carlos."

"How do you feel about that?"

"I'm thrilled. I'd be glad to see Carlos mad."

"Why does he hate Carlos so much? Because of that elopement incident?"

"It's a long story. They knew each other long ago. When we came from New Hampshire, they became fast friends. They were always together. Then something happened. I don't know what, but I think it had to do with Dr. Umber. Ben was his friend. Carlos hated him. They started hating each other. That fight was just a carry-over."

Umber again. Will that man ever stop destroying people's lives?

"Ben's been around a lot lately. Being nice, helping, bringing me coffee. You know, the usual."

Emma didn't. For her, there was no usual. She only drank coffee if she made it. She got help when she asked for it, but she'd never had to wonder if someone was trying to get into her pants.

"Of course," she said. "But doesn't it bother you that he's married? And has young kids?"

Faith shrugged.

"They are his problem. I have enough problems of my own. And I'd love to hurt Carlos."

Emma got that. She'd wished all sorts of badness upon Amber—acne, alopecia, scabies, every ugly disease, from A to Z. Still, she wouldn't date a married man for that.

"Plus, it's nice to feel wanted. Even if it's just to give Carlos a hissy fit."

"You think he cares? Even though he left you?"

"Oh, he cares all right. Just won't admit to it. Seeing me with Ben will do a number on his liver. How about you, Emma? Is there anybody you're interested in?"

Emma laughed. "I'm married to my job. That's the one thing that interests me."

"That's why you're so good. I've never met a better doctor. But it won't keep you warm at night."

"That's OK. I have a goose-down comforter." *And wine.*

Faith's luminous blue eyes bathed her in warmth. She put her hand on Emma's knee.

"You can do better."

Emma shrunk. She struggled to smile. *I'm just not used to people being nice to me. I don't know how to handle it.* She took Faith's hand to free her knee, then she dropped it, pretending to arrange her hair.

Friendship is hard!

Two days later, Emma's whole body was still hurting from the MMA class. It hurt to sit, it hurt to stand, it hurt to cough. Fortunately, the ER was busy enough to take her mind off her aches and pains. She had no time to worry about anything else but her patients. Like the woman in Room 15. She clearly hadn't been well in a while. The flesh had melted off her hollow temples, leaving just parchment skin stretched over bones. She grunted, struggling to breathe. She couldn't speak.

Emma checked the nursing-home paperwork to get her story. "Two days of fever and low oxygen. Seldom oriented. Needs help with all her activities of daily living."

What a sad existence. She can't walk, can't use the bathroom, can't feed herself. She sighed and looked for a MOLST, a document that would convey her wishes about her care. No luck. Only a power of attorney for somebody in Florida.

"I'll call them. George, let's go with the sepsis workup. Don't forget the lactate and the cultures. I'll ask Sal to start antibiotics."

"You want a gas?"

"Yep. I'll get respiratory with bipap. I'll write for steroids and breathing treatments."

"That's not going to do much," George said. "She's too far gone. She'll need intubation."

"It may buy us time to find her family. They may agree to comfort care."

"Good plan. She's suffered enough," he said, his voice cracking.

He's thinking about Mary. Her death changed him. He's still a great nurse, but he's lost the drive to just do anything to keep them alive.

"I'll do my best."

She called. No answer. She left a message and went to see her other patients. When she came back to Room 15, a large blonde woman was sitting by the bed. A heavy, sweet perfume choked the room. Emma's stomach churned.

"I'm Dr. Steele. You are...?"

"I'm her daughter. How is she?"

"I'm afraid that your mother is very sick."

"But you'll make her better. Please, do whatever you need to do to save her," the woman sobbed.

There goes comfort care.

"She's very ill. I don't know that anything we can do will make a difference."

"Are you saying she's dying?"

"She's old and sick. She hasn't been well in a long time."

"She was fine last time I saw her!"

"When was that?"

The woman took out a tissue. She wiped her eyes.

"This year? Last year?"

"It doesn't matter. You must save her! I need to speak to

her! I don't care what you have to do, just do it! I need to tell her it wasn't my fault!" Her sobs turned into wails. Staff looked in, ready to help. Emma closed the door.

"She has trouble breathing. To help her, we'd have to put a plastic tube down her throat to connect her to a breathing machine. We'd have to place a large needle in her neck to give her medications. It will hurt."

"Will it save her?"

"Save her? No. It may keep her alive a little longer. It may not. She will never be well. Most likely she'll get worse. Alternatively, we could do all we can to keep her comfortable."

"Will she live?"

"Not for long. But she'd be comfortable. She would die with dignity, and without pain. You could sit and talk to her."

"Will she answer?"

"Probably not."

"I need her to talk to me. She must forgive me."

"She won't do that," George said. "She can't speak."

"You must keep her alive. Do everything! I have the power of attorney. I'll sign for it! Where do I sign?"

"You think she would like that? To be kept alive by machines? Is that what she wanted?" George asked.

Her eyes burning, her fists clenched, the woman turned to George.

"I'll tell you what you need to do. Everything. You'll do everything to keep her alive!"

George shrugged.

"Is there anybody else we could talk to? Your siblings? Any other family?"

"I'll speak to them. I'll speak to whoever I want to! And

you, you'll do your job. You'll keep her alive! That's all you need to worry about."

Emma sighed.

"Let's see how she responds to treatment."

She's not ready. There's no point in pushing it.

38

An hour later George went on break. Carlos covered for him. On his way to checking on Room 15, he stopped by the break room to grab a coffee. He had so much trouble sleeping lately that he could barely stay awake during the day.

The note near the coffee maker read: "Fresh at 9:30." He checked his watch. 12:15. He shrugged and poured himself a cup. He was almost done when the door opened and Brenda came in. She smiled.

"How're you doing, Carlos?"

"Good. You?"

"I heard you and Faith no longer…"

"No."

"She's seeing Ben, I heard."

"You've heard a lot of things."

"One can't help it. Gossip travels in the ER like wildfire."

Carlos finished his coffee.

"Carlos?"

He stopped, his hand on the doorknob.

"How about drinks after work?"

"Sorry. I have errands to run."

"Tomorrow?"

"I have a doctor's appointment."

"Next week?"

Carlos took a deep breath. He didn't need this. He didn't want to hurt her feelings, but he had no choice. He wasn't interested in Brenda. He wasn't interested in any woman. But Faith. And his interest in Faith was a disease.

"Sorry, Brenda, I'm not ready to date. Not yet."

Brenda's smile melted.

"I'm not your type?"

"You're a very attractive woman," Carlos said, looking at his shoes.

"But not your type. You like them white, do you?"

Carlos heard his blood boil in his brain He clenched his fists but spoke softly.

"Sorry, Brenda. My personal life is personal."

"You're brown too, you know. Even if you act like you're white."

She slammed the door behind her.

He saw red. *Where the hell's that coming from? What's she talking about?*

By the time his pulse had slowed enough to let him go back, he heard: "Dr. Steele to Room 15, STAT."

That's where I was going.

He was too late.

39

After the conversation with Room 15's daughter, Emma went to see the chest pain in Room 4. He looked OK. The dog bite in Room 11 was easy. No sutures. Just cleaning and antibiotics. *And education: Don't let your child pinch the dog while she's eating. It's not rocket science!*

She stopped by Room 15. The daughter wasn't there. The patient looked much better. Good news all around. Her fingers were so cold that she couldn't get the oxygen sats. She left a note asking George to get a forehead probe. She ordered a repeat blood gas and paged the hospitalist, then moved on to her next patient.

Room 5. Three-year-old fall. The triage comment was "The family demands a head CT scan."

She went to Room 5. A crying woman sat on the stretcher holding a screaming toddler with a bruise on his forehead. A man in a white wife-beater paced the room.

Emma smiled and introduced herself. Nobody smiled back.

"Where did he fall from?"

"The shopping cart," the man said.

They feel guilty. That's why they're angry.

"Did he cry immediately?"

"Yes," the woman sobbed.

"Any vomiting?"

"No."

The kid looked great but for the frontal hematoma. Emma sang to him as she checked him out inch by inch.

"Now we try the ankle—and the knee—and the hip."

The kid laughed.

"And the belly—it doesn't hurt—it doesn't hurt—but it's ticklish..."

They all started laughing. *That's my singing voice. I'd better not quit my day job.*

They agreed to watch the kid. No CT. *We'll save a couple of grand on the workup, and save the kid a bunch of radiation.*

As she left the room, the speakers croaked: "Dr. Steele to Room 15."

She ran. George was performing CPR. The daughter got in Emma's face, howling.

"You killed her! You killed her!"

Emma stepped around her to get to the patient. She checked for a pulse. None.

"What happened?"

George, still doing CPR, answered in spurts:

"I don't know... I gave the meds to Room 6... then I went on break...when I came back...she was unresponsive."

"You killed her, you motherfuckers! She's dead!"

She's right on one account.

"I'll sue you! I'll get you fired! I'll put you in jail! You'll never see the light of day! Murderers."

They needed security to escort her out.

Epinephrine, CPR, intubation—nothing helped.

She stayed dead.

40

———

Emma wished she had a chance to stop and think. To understand what happened. Another elderly patient dying unexpectedly. This was case #5. How? Why? She didn't know. The one thing she knew was that she was toast. This was the fifth sudden death. The daughter's anger and threats were likely to be the last straw. She was done as medical director. Fortunately, she didn't have time to feel sorry for herself. She had an ER to run.

She went to run the board, checking on the new patients.

Room 14. Thirty-eight. Altered mental status.

On her way to the room, she ran through the differential diagnosis. *There has to be a reason. The elderly? Anything gets them altered. A touch of pneumonia, a urinary tract infection, forgetting their meds—or taking them twice. A 38-year-old is something else. Alcohol? Drugs? Seizure? Encephalitis? He'll need a workup.*

He didn't. She diagnosed him from the door. A textbook case for liver cirrhosis. Yellow, distended abdomen, spider veins. *Metabolic encephalopathy.*

She smiled and introduced herself. They shook hands.

"What happened?"

"I'm getting confused. My ammonia must be up."

Emma laughed. "I wish all my confused patients told me what's wrong with them. We'd save time and tons of money."

"I know. I've been here before. Your people scanned the bejesus out of me. They made me into a pincushion. They even wanted to do a spinal tap. I almost signed out against medical advice."

"You can't sign out AMA if you're altered."

"I know."

"Have you been drinking?"

"Not in six months. Ever since they told me I had cirrhosis."

"Good for you. But what makes you say you are confused?"

"Not why. Who." He nodded to the plump elderly lady coming through the door. "Dr. Steele, meet my aunt. She's the one telling me I'm losing it."

"Hi. I'm Dr. Vera Tolpeghin."

"Glad to meet you. What specialty?"

"Oh, I'm not your kind of doctor. I have a PhD in biology."

"Interesting," Emma lied.

"I can see you're fascinated."

Emma laughed.

"Never mind. He has trouble, especially in the evenings. Sundowning maybe? He gets distracted and has trouble finishing his sentences. He's fine in the morning, but the evenings are no good. I hope it's not another GI bleed."

"We'll check."

She headed out. Dr. Tolpeghin stopped her.

"We couldn't help but hear what happened next door. That woman was awful."

"She was upset," Emma said.

"She was a bitch. A raging bitch."

Emma opened her mouth. She closed it. Her nephew laughed.

"That's Vera for you. No sugarcoating, no political correctness, no nothing. You can't tell it by her accent, but she's Russian. They're not PC."

"Get over it, Boris. You're just as Russian as I am. And just as politically incorrect." She turned to Emma. "My being Russian is irrelevant. What's relevant is that I'm on the hospital board of directors. Remember that, if you ever need help. Like maybe with this bitch."

That was a first for Emma. Whenever people told her who they were, they either wanted VIP care, or tried to threaten her. Nobody had ever offered to help.

"Thank you, Dr. Tolpeghin. I appreciate it."

"Vera. And I mean it." She handed Emma her card. "You, ER folks, work so hard. You deserve more appreciation."

"Thank you...Vera."

"Enough sweet talk. Am I getting checked or what?" Boris asked.

She checked him.

"Everything looks good," Emma said, when she went to discharge him.

"Thank you."

"My pleasure."

"Are you single?" he asked. With his yellow face split by a wide smile, he looked like a jack-o'-lantern.

Emma laughed. "I don't think that's relevant."

"Why not?"

"I don't date patients."

"Once I leave the ER, I'm no longer your patient."

"I don't think so."

"Too bad. I'll be in touch. You never know. You may change your mind."

That was the best moment of her day. Even though it reminded her of the dangers of alcohol. Her diet was mostly wine-based these days. Even now, she was looking forward to her wine. Like he must have been, just months ago.

It's too late for him. His liver is gone, and his future with it.

Am I next?

41

ANGEL

This one's for you, Emma. You wanted her dead. She wanted to be dead. Even her daughter wanted her dead.

After she got absolution. No matter what it cost. What a bitch!

I know you wanted to help her across the rainbow bridge.

You can't. They'd take your license. They'd shame you. They'd put you away.

I can. I'm here for you.

For my old friend Carlos, too. Like Hannibal Lecter, I'm having an old friend for dinner.

He's already cooking.

He just doesn't know it yet.

42

That evening something had changed. Emma knew it as soon as she set foot in the house. The place was clean. No dirty dishes. Nothing on the counter. The old kitchen sparkled. That hadn't happened since Taylor came back. That hardly ever happened before that.

It can't be good. Last time I came home to a clean kitchen was when Victor left us. What the hell is it now?

It had been another bad day. Another dead patient. One could hear the daughter's screams across the lake. She threatened to sue them. Risk Management wasn't pleased. Neither was Gus. Her time was running out.

She needed wine. She grabbed a bottle. Heartland 2012. Australian Shiraz. Screw cap, like most New World wines. *Good. I don't need to look for the corkscrew.*

The bottle opened with a crack. Emma poured a good third into a long-stemmed glass. She looked through it. Dark red, opaque, earthy. She sniffed it. *Dark fruit and pepper.* Her mood lightened. She took a long sip, letting the smooth heat of the wine tickle her tongue, bathing her taste buds. She swallowed. She took a second sip. She refilled the glass. She was ready.

No music, no typing, no sobbing. She's either asleep or gone.

Taylor's door was cracked open. Emma knocked.

"Hi Mom." Taylor, beautiful and calm, sat up in bed.

Careful not to spill her wine, Emma dropped in the orange rocking chair in the corner. Rocking soothed her. She loved it, even though it was a trap. Getting out of it was a job for Houdini.

"How are you?" Emma asked.

"I've been better."

"Me too."

"What happened?"

"I lost a patient."

"Don't you lose some every day?"

"Not quite."

"You still care, after all these years?"

"Of course I care. I couldn't do my job otherwise. At least I shouldn't. If you don't care, you don't belong there. People deserve better."

"Yep, but to get upset every time they die..."

"Not every time. Sometimes it's a blessing. When it's their time to die."

"Today it wasn't?"

"I think it was."

"Then why are you upset?"

"Her daughter took it badly. And I don't understand why she died."

"Why does it matter? Who cares?"

"The hospital cares. My malpractice insurance cares. I care. I need to understand what happens to my patients. It's my job."

"Do you always worry about your job?"

"I always worry about my responsibilities. My job is one. You're another. How are you?"

"I'm better now. I thought."

"That helps." Emma sipped on the wine. She rocked. It felt good on her back.

"I thought about myself."

How unusual.

"And?"

"I spoke to Eric. He didn't take it well."

"What did he say?"

"He left."

"He must have been surprised. He needs time."

"He ran away."

"I'm sorry, Taylor."

"You told me."

For once, Taylor wasn't having a crisis, though she was due. She didn't even blame Emma. *Growing up, maybe?*

"I spoke to Dad."

"What did he say?"

"He said that true love never dies. If Eric loves me, he'll come back."

Emma swallowed her remark about Victor and true love with another sip of wine.

"Would you take him back?"

"Of course. If you love him. He needs time to get used to the idea."

"No. Not Eric. Would you take Dad back?"

Shit.

"Taylor, he left ten years ago. He's married. He has kids. There's nothing to take back."

"If he came and asked, would you take him back?"

Not in a thousand years.

"I don't think that's something to worry about."

"I'm not worried. I'm hopeful!"

"Taylor, don't you have enough to think about? You, the baby, Eric? Victor's got Amber, the kids, and the dogs. He's all set."

"How about you? Who do you have?"

"I have you. And I have my work."

"Your work has you. The ER owns you. You need to get a life. You need somebody. I have my own life. I'm going to be gone soon. As soon as I figure out what to do with myself."

"Thanks, Taylor, but don't worry about me. Let's think about you."

"I need a job. I need to make myself useful, instead of laying here, feeling sorry for myself."

Wow. "How about college?

"In a year or two. Maybe. After the baby's born. And I grow up a little."

"What job are you thinking about?"

"I want to work in the hospital."

"Why?"

"You're a doctor. Dad's a doctor. Eric is a nurse. Everybody close to me is into medicine, one way or another. I want to see if that's my thing."

"That makes sense." Emma said, hoping she'd change her mind. Taylor in the hospital? What a disaster! She didn't like taking orders. *And that's what we all do there. Everyone, from the environmental workers to the CEO. We take stupid orders. Patients, consultants, insurance companies, lawyers, the government. They're all riding us.*

"What are you going to do?" Taylor asked.

"Me?"

"Yes. What are you going to do about your life?" Taylor's gaze bore into her.

She's taken me on as a project! God forbid she decides I need to take Victor back!

"I'll get a dog."

The thought came out of nowhere. Her heart sang. She smiled.

I'll get a dog. That's exactly what I need. Better than men, healthier than wine.

43

Carlos couldn't find a working IV pump. He tried Room 23, then 25. Nothing. He went to 26. He heard moans. Somebody in pain? He opened the door. The IV pump was there.

So was Ben. Lying sideways across the stretcher, his scrub bottoms around his ankles. His coarse face was tight, his jaw clenched. Impaling herself on top of him, Faith smiled, her indigo eyes hazed with pleasure.

Carlos felt sick.

He bolted out, slamming the door. He barely made it to the bathroom across the hall. He retched again and again until he was empty. He felt weak. He splashed cold water over his face. His teeth chattering, he sat on the toilet to recover. He heard the door.

"What if he talks?" Ben asked.

"He won't. Why would he?"

"To sink us. If they find out, we're toast. Our jobs are over. My marriage's down the drain."

"Your marriage was down the drain already."

"Common, Faith! What was I supposed to tell you? My

wife's busy with the twins and I feel horny? I want a bit on the side? You know better!"

"So, your marriage..."

"It's fine. As long as he doesn't talk."

Faith laughed. A chill ran down Carlos's spine.

"Make sure he doesn't talk, then."

"How?"

"Find a way."

"I will. One way or another, I will." Their voices faded.

Weak again, Carlos lay on the floor.

Faith. And Ben.

Together. Against him.

44

E mma forgot her wine. *Breed: Any. Size: Any. Area: Northeast. Age: Any. Color: Color?! What's wrong with people? What does color have to do with anything? It's not a wig.*

Taylor isn't excited about the dog. Too bad.

Emma loved dogs. From the mutt she'd had as a kid, to Thelma and Louise, the two Bichons. Victor took them when he left and left her Taylor.

What a deal.

She was getting a dog. Her own. Somebody to share her life with. *I'd like somebody to miss me. It's selfish, I know. Still, it would be nice to have somebody missing me, for once. Somebody to miss me, not the things I can do for them.*

She found puppies. Her heart swelled.

I should get a dog from the pound. They sit there like second-hand merchandise, hoping for someone to take them home. They need a second chance. Don't we all?

But...... she'd always wanted a German Shepherd. They were the kings of dogs. Smart, loyal, strong, beautiful. She loved that in a dog. She'd love that in a man too, but they didn't have those at the pound. Nor anywhere else, apparently.

How about rescuing a German Shepherd? She typed in "GSD rescue."

Puppies. Heart-melting, thick-legged, floppy-eared, black and tan German Shepherd puppies.

She had no time for a puppy. She barely had time to brush her teeth. *A puppy needs time, love, and commitment. Two out of three isn't good enough.* She typed "shepherd rescue."

Amber eyes looked at her from a Facebook post. Long face. Long hair. Dark. *"Her owner died. She needs a home without other dogs. No cats. No young children. She needs a knowledgeable owner, a fenced yard, and a commitment to training."*

The post was three months old. The dog was hundreds of miles away. A beautiful dog in a wire cage. The pictures were taken through the wire. Long dark coat. Ferocious white teeth. Haunting eyes.

Not a happy dog.

Emma called.

"Yes, she's still available." The voice was bored. They'd been through this before. "You'll have to sign that you take responsibility for any damages, injuries, or deaths."

Deaths?

They didn't want money or references. She was four. Her owner left some money for her care. It was running out. They'd been looking for months now. They may have to put her down. Yes, tomorrow morning was OK.

Emma had a day off. If she left now, she'd get there in the morning, and be back tomorrow for dinner. She opened the fridge. Empty. Taylor had eaten it. She tried the freezer.

Bread. Frozen broccoli. Spaghetti sauce, heavy on the garlic. Nothing else. *It will have to do.*

She drove for hours in the rain. The glare burned her eyes. She missed a turn. That added another hour. By the time she got there, the sky was blushing pink. She pulled on the side of the road and curled up in the back seat.

She woke up late. She guzzled her cold coffee. She needed to pee. She wanted to brush her teeth. No time, no place.

Oh well. Fuck them if they can't take a joke!

She grabbed the spaghetti sauce and scrambled out of the car. She tried to unbend. Slow going. *I'm too old for this. If only I had some Motrin.*

She straightened up all the way and rang the doorbell.

"You're late," the fat man said. His small pig eyes matched his pink Hawaiian shirt.

"Sorry. I fell asleep."

He appraised her. "You know dogs?"

"Somewhat."

"Police dogs?"

"No."

"This is no ordinary dog."

"How so?"

"She's a police dog. She took a bullet in a drug raid. In the lung. She never got back to normal. They say she has PTSD. They retired her."

"How did you end up with her?"

"My brother wanted a protection dog. He got her when the police got rid of her."

"What happened to him?"

"He died."

"How?"

"A business partner shot him."

"She couldn't protect him?"

"She's fast, but bullets are faster. But the guy will never walk again."

Emma shuddered.

"You still want to see her?"

"Yes."

He pointed to the door at the end of the hallway. "In there."

"What's her name?"

"Guinness."

Emma looked at the closed door. She'd driven the whole night to get here. She could just turn around and go home, or she could open the door. *The absence of fear is not courage. That's stupidity. Courage is feeling the fear and doing it anyhow. Or maybe that's stupidity.* She opened the door. The morning sun poured in her eyes, making the room dark. She shielded her eyes with her hand.

"Guinness?"

Unblinking yellow eyes in the far corner.

"Hi, Guinness."

Emma stepped in. She sat on the stool by the door. The eyes watched.

"How're you doing?"

Nothing.

She doesn't feel like chatting.

Emma looked for something to say. Nothing came. She was stiff and hungry. She needed to pee. She had driven forever to get here, and she had to drive back. The dog didn't seem to care.

"Life sucks." Emma rested her back on the wall. "I have a long drive back. I'd better find a toilet and something to eat first."

Curled up, her dark nose resting on bronze paws, the dog listened. *She gets it.*

"I'm sorry your life sucks. Mine sucks too, you know. My daughter hates my guts. My ex-husband got bored with his pretty wife. I think somebody's killing my patients. You think you have it rough?" Emma looked at her watch.

"I have another shift tomorrow. My daughter is more trouble than any puppy." She looked the dog in the eye.

"Ever had puppies, Guinness?"

The dog didn't blink. Emma shrugged.

"You didn't miss much. They're a pain in the ass. Once you have them, life's never the same. Trust me."

The dog seemed doubtful.

"You're right. Why should you trust me? I'm just a stranger. You must miss your human. Your owner, they said. Like you can own somebody! You don't even own your kids. There's this joke. A woman gets fed up with her kids and decides to sell them on eBay. She tells her friend. He laughs. 'eBay? Are you crazy? You made them yourself! Sell them on Etsy!'"

The dog didn't laugh.

She's got a German sense of humor.

Emma crossed her legs. *I need a bathroom.* She could ask pig man, but she didn't want to use his bathroom.

It's getting late. The dog isn't interested. She doesn't even have a sense of humor.

Emma stood up. She rolled her shoulders.

"I'll go now... Sorry it didn't work out. You'll be all right. They won't put you to sleep, you have money ... unless pig man gets to keep it... that sucks."

The yellow eyes didn't blink.

She's beautiful. All dark but for the tan legs. Wise, golden eyes.

"I'm sorry. I wish I could help." She picked up her bag. It was heavy. She remembered the Bolognese.

"You like Italian? It has lots of basil and garlic. Garlic is a vermicide, you know. It kills worms. Not saying you have them, just telling you what it's good for."

She moved closer. The dog watched. Emma opened the Bolognese and sat it by the water dish.

"Good luck, old girl."

Emma wanted to pet the dog, but the dog didn't look like she wanted petting. Emma respected that. She walked out without looking back. She climbed in her car. Her eyes burned. *So much for gut feelings. Crying is for sissies, Mother said.* She set the navigator to "Home," then remembered she needed a toilet. She changed it to the nearest McDonald's.

She glanced back.

The dog. Staring at her, one inch from the window.

She opened the back door. The dog jumped in. She curled up in the back seat. She sighed. She wiggled to make herself comfortable. She sighed again. She looked at Emma. Her tail thumped.

"What are we waiting for?"

"Really?"

Guinness wagged her tail.

"McDonald's?"

Guinness smiled.

"OK."

Back in the ER for her next shift, Emma struggled to keep up. It was not a good day. Five psychiatric patients on hold, waiting for a place to go. No beds upstairs, so the ER had to hold admitted patients. Two nurses called in sick, making them short-staffed. The shit was pouring like rain. Emma hoped it wouldn't drown her.

Then Mike called her for a meeting.

"What's it about?"

"Quality."

She was in the middle of a crisis. The drunk in Room 6 had pushed the stretcher across the door, taking himself hostage. There was no ambulance to transfer the brain bleed to neurosurgery.

Now this. Whatever it is, it's not good news. He's not calling to congratulate me. It's got to be about the woman in 15 whose daughter complained. I still don't know what happened.

She talked to the charge nurse about getting a helicopter to fly out the brain bleed, hoped the drunk would fall asleep, and went to the conference room. She found them waiting. Mike, Sal, the Risk Manager, the Quality Control director, George, Carlos, the lawyer, and Gus.

"Thank you for joining us, Dr. Steele," Mike said.

You'd be late too if you had to work with patients. All of you, in fact. Sitting in your office all day makes you feel superior. You're complacent and out of touch.

"We met to discuss a few issues that occurred in our ED lately. Over the last few weeks, our mortality has increased. We have also encountered a number of sentinel events."

The quality director, a thin man with a skimpy white beard, started a PowerPoint presentation. He lusted over graphs and pie charts. Patients seen in the last thirty days. Left without being seen. AMA. Deaths. Near-deaths.

I wonder if I ordered the labs for Room 10.

"Emma!" They stared at her. "What's your take on this?"

"We have a number of separate incidents. They involve unrelated patients. The patients were here for different reasons. All, with one exception, were old and impaired. These incidents happened on different days, in different rooms, on different shifts. The patients had different doctors and nurses. We have no clear explanation of why these people died."

"And?" Gus asked.

"I thought the first one was a medication error, but there've been too many. There's only one possible explanation. I think we have a mercy killer."

If she was looking to impress them, she succeeded. They started talking all over each other.

"Preposterous idea! This couldn't happen in this hospital. This is a nice place. A quiet place, with good people. Saying something like that was an insult. She's lost her mind. Inconceivable."

Emma waited for the ruckus to calm down. She looked

them in the eye, one by one. "Remember February?"

Silence. Only months before, a slew of deaths had hit their community and their hospital. The culprit had been a shocker.

"Lightning doesn't strike twice in the same place," Mike said.

"Maybe it's the same lightning."

"He's in jail," Gus said. "He'll be there for a long time."

"Maybe he has friends. Or maybe we're just unlucky."

"You may have a point." George shuddered. February had been rough on him.

"Impossible," Mike said. "We need to look at our practices. We need to stop giving verbal orders. We need to improve monitoring. We should round on the patients more often—in every case the patient appeared stable. They were left unattended, and then found dead. If we monitored them correctly, we may be able to detect changes before it's too late."

"We need to improve the pharmacy security," Sal said. "Right now, it's easy for anybody to take meds arriving by tube for somebody else. They can just grab and use them. People can even take medications out of the locked drawers without signing for them."

"Who can do that?" the quality director asked.

"Anyone passing by the tube system," Sal said. "Especially the nurses. They can get into the med room. The pharmacists too. The pharmacy techs, who refill the meds."

"So, then what happens to the meds? They get given to the wrong patients or in the wrong amount. You're getting back to the idea of a killer," Carlos said.

"That's impossible. Nobody in my ED would do something of the kind." Mike turned red, his jaw muscle twitching.

He's about to blow up. Why is he so angry? Because it's his ED. His ED has to be perfect. Nothing bad can happen in it.

"What do we do?" Gus, the VPM, asked.

"How about speaking to the police?" the quality director said.

"NO!" Mike, Gus, and the lawyer chorused.

"Absolutely not!" the lawyer said. "That would be a disaster. Everybody who ever died here would sue us. Their families, I mean. Our reputation would be destroyed. People would be afraid to come here. They'd say we're crawling with serial killers. We'd go bankrupt!"

Gus agreed.

"We'll investigate. We'll create a special committee to research these cases and evaluate the systems. It has to be somebody who's not involved with any of the cases, of course. That excludes you, Emma; also Sal, George, and Carlos. Mike, Lola, and I will look at it."

"Who's Lola?" Emma asked.

"I am." The lawyer's mouth was a thin line. She didn't look pleased.

She doesn't know how anything works. She knows nothing about medicine. That's going to be a hit.

Emma shrugged. Not like she needed any more work, but she was going to investigate herself. She had already started. She hadn't found much, except that both Carlos and George were involved with two of the cases. A coincidence, but they were both a little off, lately. George mourned Mary and Carlos missed Faith. Still... she had to start somewhere. She'd check the schedule to see if they were working during any of the other cases. It would be nice to rule them out. And then? She had no idea. She'd make it up, as usual. The good news: her month was almost over.

One way or another, I'll be done soon.

Taylor woke up early that morning. Something felt odd. *Somebody's watching me.* She looked around. Nothing. Just her old bedroom, with the grass lamp, the starfish comforter, and the orange rocker in the corner. She rolled on her other side and went back to sleep.

Somebody's watching me.

She was in her room, alone. She was losing it. She sat up and rubbed her eyes, looking for her Crocs with her feet.

Something touched her. She jumped. A dog. A big dark dog. Staring at her.

Really?

Yep. Really. He lay there at the foot of the bed, staring at her. She stared back.

The dog didn't blink. This was a serious dog. A police dog? How did it get in the house? What was it doing there?

Mother said she was getting a dog. She did.

She'd been gone the whole day. She had a shift today—she kept a copy of her godforsaken schedule on the fridge. Somehow, in between, she had acquired this animal. Then she'd gone to work and left the dog for Taylor to deal with.

Taylor loved Thelma and Louise. She'd grown up with them. They were cute and cuddly, even though they yapped a lot. But this dog was different. It acted like a person.

Oh well. It's Mother's problem.

Taylor found her Crocs. She went to get something to eat. Now that her morning sickness was over, she was always starved. Thankfully, she was slim and burned calories like crazy. Still, she felt like a hippopotamus. She was getting slower and thicker, but she was still always hungry.

She opened the fridge. Mustard, ketchup, mayo, milk. *Like really? Not even eggs? How's a growing woman supposed to handle this?*

She found a box of Cheerios. That would have to do. Lunch looked like a losing proposition unless she got her ass out to do some shopping.

Where's the new you? The new you who'll get a job, grow up, and become responsible?

Taylor flipped the bird to that thought. She grabbed the Cheerios and a box of Oreos. She poured Cheerios, lots of sugar, and milk in a bowl and grabbed a spoon. She dropped on the sofa and turned on the TV.

The dog sat in front of her, staring. His head obstructed the screen.

"What?" Taylor said.

The dog gurgled. It wasn't a bark and it wasn't a growl.

"What do you want?"

The dog gurgled again, staring at her bowl.

He's hungry. We have no dog food. We have no food, period. Thanks, Mom!

"We have no dog food," she informed him. She took a spoon of Cheerios.

The dog gurgled again. Staring her in the face, the dog clearly demanded to eat.

"Don't you get it? We have no..." The dog looked at her bowl like Taylor would look at a fudge Sunday.

He wants my Cheerios. Dogs don't eat people food!

She lifted the spoon to her mouth. The dog drooled, watching its progression like it was the Olympics. Taylor opened her mouth. She closed it.

"Fine. Be that way. They got soggy anyhow!" She put the bowl on the floor next to the sofa. "You happy now?"

The dog stared at her.

"What?"

The dog stared.

"What are you staring at me for? Eat it!"

The dog gave a short happy bark and cleaned the bowl in a blink. He sat in front of it and gave a quick bark. He looked at Taylor and wagged his tail. Once.

"Thanks." He went to lie down by the door.

Taylor scratched her head.

She got herself another bowl of cereal and watched for the dog to come back. He didn't.

She finished her cereal and went to clean up. Brushed her teeth, took a shower, got dressed.

The dog waited by the door.

He needs to go out.

There was no leash—they hadn't had a dog in years. Taylor found a soft belt. She walked slowly toward the dog. She wasn't sure he cared to be touched.

"Want to go out?"

The dog wagged his tail.

She slipped the loop of the belt over his head. She tightened it. He didn't seem to mind. She opened the door. The dog waited. For what?

"Let's go," Taylor said. The dog leapt out. He smelled the bushes, the stones, and the grass. He squatted at the gate.

"You're a girl!"

The dog looked at her and smiled. They took a long walk. Taylor hadn't done that ever since she'd tried to kill herself. She was surprised to see it was still spring. It felt like ages ago.

Back home, Taylor removed the belt. The dog looked at her. She scratched her behind the ears. The dog smiled again.

Back in the bedroom, her phone rang. She had forgotten her phone. Unbelievable. She never forgot her phone. Five missed calls. One was Mother, one was Father, three were Eric.

"Call me."

They're screwed up, these people. There's something wrong with their lives. The Shaman needs help. That's why I came with her. Her spaghetti sauce? Pulleaze! You'd better rub it on against vampires and mosquitoes than eat it! But she's OK.

Why Shaman? She smells like healing and dark magic. She knows things others don't.

On the way home we stopped at McDonald's. She ran out of the car as if she chased someone. I got ready to help her. But no, she just needed to pee. That's the problem with humans. Women, especially. Men—they'd go for a nice bush, but women? They're crazy about toilet paper. Can't imagine why. I tried it. It's not good. It tastes just like cardboard.

She came back more together. She brought a couple of Big Macs and an order of fries. Not my favorite, I'd rather go for a Bacon Quarter Pounder, but she tried. I licked her hands to show my appreciation. Greasy and salty. They tasted good.

It took us forever to get to her den. It smells like her. And the girl. The girl is trouble. I know trouble when I smell it. And she's not even in heat.

A few man smells. Not many. A coward, I think. Then another one, a while ago. Both running away. But I digress. There was no dog bed, so I slept in the armchair.

This morning Shaman microwaved some frozen waffles. She poured butter over them. Never had waffles before. Not bad, especially if you haven't eaten in a week. I didn't feel like it.

OK, OK, I was worried they'd poison me. Yes, I could smell it, but still. How would you eat if you were on death row?

She left me a bowl of water and told me to be quiet. I looked for the girl. I found her. She looked at me as if I wasn't real.

Oh, girl, I'm real, all right. Your stuff isn't real. All those things you ruminate about. We eat, we love, we shit, we die. That's all there is to it.

She came around a little, but she needs a lot of work. They both do. What's wrong with people? As long as you're together, you're OK. Stop thinking about all these maybes and maybe not and such nonsense. I'm glad I'm not people.

The doorbell. I jump off the sofa, where we're watching TV as she's scratching my ears. I rush to the door.

"Back off!"

The girl grabs my collar and opens the door. A man. Shocked. He stares at me. Stares at her belly. Stares at me. She jumps in his arms, crying.

I growl. She turns around and tells me he's OK.

"Then why are you crying?"

She cries some more. They hold each other and kiss. It's gross. They sit on MY sofa! Humans! I watch them.

"This is Eric," *she says, amongst tears.*

I give him a paw to shake. They stare at me. They laugh. Eric shakes.

"Hello...What's his name?"

"She's a girl."

"Oh. What's her name?"

She looks at me. She doesn't know. She texts her mother.

"Guinness. Her name is Guinness. Hi, Guinness!"

I give her my paw again. She shakes it. They laugh. What's so funny?

Whatever. It beats crying!

48

After squaring away the brain bleed and the drunk and the other challenges of another lousy shift, Emma sat in her office.

She finally got to think about the quality meeting. Her jaw clenched, she started fuming. They told her to mind her own business! As her patients died in her ER. Inconceivable.

She logged in the computer to have another look at the charts. She had perused them so many times that her eyes started glazing over them. To focus, she started a list, looking for similarities.

Death #1. Monday, April 9. Room 5.

Patient: Old nursing home patient with hip fracture.

Doctor: Alex. Nurse: Brenda.

Mechanism: Unknown. *Opiate overdose, maybe? The woman's vitals got better just before she died. Opiates would give her pain relief and normalize her vitals. At first. Then they'd put her to sleep. For good.*

Coroner's report: Pulmonary edema. The toxicology report was still pending. *She got morphine, so she's going to be positive for opiates no matter what. Carlos worked that day.*

George didn't. That doesn't mean much. He could stop by, for one reason or another. We all do. For a meeting, to return a book, whatever.

Death #2. Wednesday, April 11. Room 20.

Patient: Old woman with dehydration and rash.

Doctor: Kurt. Nurse: Carlos.

Mechanism: Hypoglycemia. *Insulin? Maybe that ordered for another patient?* She wrote herself a note: Who took out that insulin? Who gave it? When? Ask Sal.

Coroner's report: Nothing. Tox report is pending. *This one may help. An abnormal C-peptide will confirm that she received insulin she had no business getting.*

Case # 3. Saturday, April 14. Unknown room. *This one didn't die.*

Patient: Old woman with a urinary tract infection. Discharged back to the nursing home. Returned next day with severe unexplained dehydration.

Mechanism: *Lasix overdose? That would make her pee a lot. That would get her dehydrated. Would anyone notice at the nursing home? The urinary tract infection made her pee a lot anyhow. Hypertonic saline? That would scar the vein. But whoever gave it didn't give a damn. Dead people don't need veins.*

Doctor: Alex. Nurse: Ben.

Coroner's report: None yet.

Death #4. Sunday, April 15. Room 5.

Patient: Middle-aged man with back pain.

Doctor: Me. Nurse: Carlos.

Coroner's report: Not yet.

Mechanism: *Who knows? Maybe I missed a dissection or an aneurysm. I almost hope it's that, rather than someone killing a healthy patient. My patient! But if they did, how? The meds I wrote for him were removed from the pixies. Carlos says he left them on the counter. Did anyone give them? But they weren't enough to kill him anyhow.*

A knock at the door. Emma threw her notes in the drawer and minimized her computer screen. She'd been told to mind her own business. She didn't want to get caught detecting. Not before she found the answers.

"Come in."

Faith came in, glowing and full of life, filling her scrubs in all the right places. Her warm indigo blue eyes embraced Emma.

"You're still here?"

"Catching up on some work. How are you, Faith?"

"I'm good. You?"

"Hanging in there. This work is beating me lately."

"I bet. All these deaths."

Emma cleared her voice. "What's up, Faith? What can I do for you?"

"I wondered if you'd like to go for a hike on Tuesday? Or maybe to a spa?"

"I'd love to, but I can't, Faith. Not until I catch up a little."

"Who do you think is killing all these people?"

"I don't know. I don't think anybody does."

"Well, they are dying!"

"Is there anything I can do for you, Faith?"

Faith's smile faded. "I'll let you be. I can see you're busy. Let me know if you have some time and want to do something."

The door slammed shut. *I must have hurt her feelings. I'm sorry. I'll talk to her tomorrow.*

Death #5: Thursday, April 18. Room 15.

Patient: *That was the demented patient with pneumonia whose daughter wanted everything done. She looked better after treatment, then she coded. What a mess that was.*

Doctor: *Me again.* Nurse: George. Relieved by Carlos.
Mechanism: *Who the hell knows?*
Autopsy: Pending.
Case #6?

No Case #6. Not yet. *The way things are going, there'll be one soon.* Five cases in less than a month. She had no proof that they were related. Some may have been unrelated. Natural deaths. Accidents.

Still, four died. Two of them were hers. The back pain and the pneumonia. That was weird. Different nurses, different rooms, different meds.

What did they all have in common?

1. They were all old, impaired, demented nursing-home patients. Except for the back pain.
2. They all seemed to be medication related. There were no stabbings, no shootings... But...she remembered Alex's case, the old smoker on bipap he had had to intubate. He got detached from the vent. *Shit. That's six. Case six already happened. I need to find out more.*
3. None of them was anywhere close to dying.
4. There was no family present, except for the blind husband of the hypoglycemia and the irate daughter of her pneumonia patient.
5. None screamed, or asked for help. In fact, they all looked better just before getting dead.

That's it. I don't know where to go from here. If there's anything they have in common, it's me. I had two of them, and I was there for two more. What the hell does that mean? And the back pain? That one doesn't fit. Maybe that's where the answer is.
She made a list.

1. Get data about Alex's bipap case.
2. The insulin.
3. Who gave the meds to the back pain?
4. The back pain is an outlier. What if he's the only target and the others just obfuscate? Did he have an enemy in the ER? An ex-wife? A rival? A competitor?

Her head was spinning. She was ravenous. She had to check on Taylor. She grabbed her coat.

Shit! I have a dog! I hope Taylor let her out! And gave her something to eat! I was going to text Taylor. I forgot!

She flew out the door.

49

Carlos watched the patient in Room 2 like a hawk. Bad things kept happening to his patients. He wasn't going to let this one go bad on him.

The old man had smoked his last cigarette. His bony chest heaving, he sat up propped on his arms to get more air. He fought hard, but he wasn't winning. He was on continuous nebs, he'd already received steroids, magnesium —the whole kit and caboodle, but he wasn't going anywhere good.

His oxygen sats dropped. Carlos turned the oxygen all the way up.

"Let's prepare to intubate," Dr. Crump said, chewing on his lip.

He didn't want to intubate. The man was already hypoxic. His CO_2 was through the roof. The few seconds he had to be without ventilation could be enough to stop his heart. But they didn't have a choice.

The respiratory therapist took over the mask. Carlos went to the locked medication room to get the RSI kit, the sealed bag of intubation drugs. He opened it and waited for orders.

"Thirty of etomidate, then ten of vecuronium," Dr. Crump said. He turned to the RT: "Let's have the nasal canula at 15 liters for apneic oxygenation."

Carlos pushed the drugs. One minute later, the patient stopped breathing. Smooth as silk, Dr. Crump slid the tube in. The oxygen saturation stayed unchanged. The RT started bagging. The sats went up.

Carlos sighed. *Thank God. Maybe the evil spirits following me got the day off today.*

He'd been having a rough time lately. First, the back-pain guy. He took out the meds but never gave them. Then the guy died and the meds disappeared. That bugged him ever since. That, and the feeling that someone was watching him. It was unsettling. Dr. Steele watched him too. She double-checked his meds. She followed him in patients' rooms. Even George was getting weird. He went to bed early. No more sitting and chatting. It was like a heavy cloud hung over him. Always waiting for something bad to happen. *Not today.*

He grabbed the blood vials to send them to the lab. He stopped by the pixies to get another breathing treatment for his patient. He came back and rechecked the vitals. Everything looked OK, except for the RSI kit.

The RSI kit was gone.

50

T hat morning Emma woke up to Guinness staring at her. One tail thump.

"Good morning."

"Good morning. We have the day off."

Guinness thumped her tail again.

"What would you like to do?"

Guinness smiled.

"After breakfast."

She smiled wider.

I've never seen a dog smile before. Her eyes shine, her mouth's wide open, her pink tongue's reaching her knees. And those teeth. I'm glad I'm not her dental tech.

Emma went to the fridge. The dog followed.

Empty. So much for breakfast! No dog food either.

"McDonald's?"

Tail thump. Emma opened the car door. The dog stared.

"OK."

Guinness jumped in. Emma closed the door and climbed in to find Guinness in the front seat. *There now, as the surgeons say instead of Oops! I guess she's not a back-seat person.*

Emma put on her seat belt. Guinness stared at her.

"What?"

One bark.

"You want the seat belt?

Bark.

Emma shrugged. She bent over to click her seat belt. It didn't fit well.

"I'll get you a leash, a bed, and a seat belt. And dog food. You can't live on fast food forever."

"Why not?" Guinness cocked her head.

They shared the Egg McMuffins, but Guinness declined the coffee. They went to the pet store. Guinness chose a black collar with shiny metal spikes and a six-foot long, heavy leash.

"I didn't know you were into Goth."

Guinness pretended not to hear. She inspected the dog food and settled for a hypoallergenic rice and lamb formula.

Their shopping done, they drove to the park. An over-grown old farm crisscrossed by trails between rocky lakeshores, the park was a joy to explore. Guinness checked the doggie mail. She squatted over rocks. She spotted squirrels in the trees and chipmunks under logs. She ran away. She came back. She ran again.

"You love your freedom."

Emma did too. She felt lighter than she had in a long time. She forgot the ER, the deaths, Taylor, Victor. She forgot everything but the blooming trees, the breeze singing through the branches, the heavy scent of moist earth and spring. Emma delighted in the beauty of nature and in Guinness's undemanding company. The dog understood things without being told and had no expectations—beyond breakfast. They played frisbee. Guinness went swimming, then shook, giving Emma a shower. They laughed.

The phone rang.

They needed her in the ER. They had a mass casualty incident. A school bus had hit a truck, then rolled over in the river. Two died at the scene. The rest were on their way.

51

B ack in Room 2, Carlos had to hold on to the counter to stay upright. He felt faint and sick to his stomach. His heart pounded in his head like a hammer.

The RSI kit was gone. He left it on the counter and went to send the labs. *Five minutes ago. Now it's gone.*

He checked the patient. He was alive. He repeated his vitals. They were OK. But the kit was gone. Full of everything, but the vecuronium and the etomidate they had used for intubation. Sedatives, putting people to sleep. Opiates. Ketamine. Paralytics, paralyzing every muscle in the body but the heart. Every one of them dangerous. Every one of them lethal.

A single dose of succinylcholine is enough to paralyze you. You wouldn't be able to move. You couldn't breathe. You couldn't scream for help. You'd watch yourself die. Same with the rocuronium. All in all, there's enough stuff there to kill half a dozen people.

He had taken the kit out under his ID and he had signed for it. Now he had lost it. He was already in trouble after losing the meds for the back pain. This was bad news.

If they find out. What if they don't? I can just sign that I discarded them. Nobody knows.

But what if whoever took the kit uses the meds to kill someone?

They won't. They only took them to get high. They'll just use the fentanyl, the ketamine, and the propofol. They'll throw away the rest. What else could they do with them?

Carlos snuck to the med room. Nobody there. He hesitated. *I shouldn't do this. But I have no choice. I can't tell them that I lost the kit.* He charted the meds as discarded. The paralytics, the ketamine, the propofol, the lot. He logged out and sighed with relief. He was done. He went to the bathroom to splash cold water over his face, and looked in the mirror. He looked terrible.

Then he remembered the cameras in the med room and broke into a cold sweat.

52

From the park, Emma drove straight to the ER. She locked Guinness in her office and went to work. The ER was in overdrive. They had lined the hallways with the existing patients to make room for the traumas. That gave them more empty rooms, but it set the visitors free to wander in the hallways and get in everybody's way.

The wounded arrived every which way: by ambulance, by private car, on foot. Scared parents came looking for their children. Volunteers came to help. The waiting room was clogged. Harried staff moved from one patient to the next, checking pulses, holding pressure on bleeding wounds, giving reassurance.

Triage had moved to the ambulance bay. *Good. Triage is not a place, it's a process.*

Ann and Kurt rocked. They glanced at patients, treating the sick, sending the others to waiting areas. The first case was already in the OR. Two more were waiting.

The whole hospital came to help. Environmental workers cleaned the rooms. Father Murphy comforted families in the waiting room. The residents looked for something to do. The place roared like a Boeing 747 on takeoff, fueled by the adrenaline rush.

Judy and Ben triaged, calling the docs for emergencies. Emma assigned them two residents to help. *The kids are awesome, but they don't have fifty years of ER experience like those two have between them. They'll learn a lot today.*

She went to check on the old patients. Ann and Kurt were too busy with the traumas to get a chance to reassess them. She tried to clear the hallways, inviting the visitors to the waiting room. They stared at her and resisted. *It's the jeans and the hoodie. I wish I had my white coat! As always, the clothes are more important than the person.* She called Security to escort a particularly reluctant couple. She moved from stretcher to stretcher, checking vitals, handing out water, making sure they stayed alive.

She stopped by Room 3. An intubated patient. A kid, whiter than his sheets. Monitors alarmed like a pinball machine. She couldn't get his blood pressure or his oxygen sat. She tried to listen to his lungs, but the disposable bedside stethoscope didn't work. *What a piece of shit! Taylor had better stethoscopes in her toddler's doctor kit.*

The beeping stopped just as she bent over him to check for a pulse. The crazy zig-zag on the monitor gave way to a straight line. The heart had stopped. *He's in asystole.* Emma hit the code button to call for help. She looked at him, trying to figure out what happened. She knew nothing about him, except that he was intubated. And young. And dead.

Out of nowhere, her frozen brain replayed the voice of Ghazala, her mentor. That pediatric airway lecture, she'd listened to it a dozen times.

"People say: If an intubated patient arrests, think DOPE: Displaced tube, Oxygen, Pneumothorax, Equipment. I disagree.

DOPE isn't cool. The families don't like it either. You standing there, looking at their loved one, mumbling DOPE, DOPE. You look like a dope. Think POET. That's a nice mnemonic. Better than DOPE."

POET. Pneumothorax, Oxygen, Equipment, Tube. Let's see.

The tube looked OK. The oxygen was on. She detached the tube from the ventilator to check it. The vent worked. She laid her hands on his chest, pressing with all her weight to force out the trapped air. Nothing.

The room filled with help.

She untied the endotracheal tube, deflated the balloon, then pulled it out of the airway. The tube looked patent. Judy took over the airway and started bagging. Amy got ready for CPR.

The trachea may be a little to the left. A tension pneumothorax? Air outside the lungs, creating so much pressure that the blood can't return to the heart. That's deadly, unless you decompress it fast.

I hope he's lucky.

"Scalpel."

Emma uncovered the right chest. She pulled on sterile gloves. A scalpel landed in her right hand.

Somebody splashed iodine on the chest, baking the white skin to brown.

Emma bent over, looking for the right spot.

"What do you think you're doing?"

Ann.

Emma didn't look up. She didn't have time.

"This is my patient!" Ann shrieked.

Emma found the space. *Anterior axillary line, just lateral to the nipple.* With her left index she found the soft space between the ribs.

"Let go of him!"

Emma opened the scalpel. She took a deep breath and cut into the chest. The silver blade went through skin like butter. She made a long cut. *An inch and a half. This isn't the time for pretty. This is the time for fast.*

Blood oozed. Fat glistened yellow, exposing dark red muscle. *I need a clamp.*

No time. Her finger punctured the flesh between the ribs to break the pleura and release the air. The flesh resisted. Emma pushed harder.

The pleura, the thin membrane lining the chest, broke with a pop. *Like a champagne cork.*

Air burst out around her finger. She pulled her finger out. Warm blood sprayed her face.

The chest was decompressed. The heart restarted.

Emma straightened. Ann's eyes, dark embers in a ghostly face, burned into hers.

She'll never forgive me for this.

"Your patient."

53

Taylor woke up smiling that morning. She felt happy for no reason. Then she remembered that Eric was back, and the day got even brighter.

They had talked about everything and nothing. About the past, the present, and the future. They learned new things about each other.

"I'll be a better lover. You need to tell me what makes you happy," he said.

"What are you talking about?"

"I'll try to be enough for you."

Then it dawned on her. He thought she had been with other men while dating him. She didn't know whether to laugh or to cry. She did both.

"I love you, Eric. You. Nobody else. This happened way before we met. I didn't tell you, since I didn't want to lose you. That was wrong. I'm sorry."

He held her like he was never going to let go.

"I don't need anyone else but you. I love you. But I'm pregnant. I'm responsible for this child who didn't ask to be born. I did drugs. I don't know what that did to the kid. But it doesn't matter. Whether he's normal or not, this is my kid. At least until I bring it into the world."

"And then?"

"I don't know. I struggle with that. Keep it? Give it up for adoption? I don't know."

"I love you."

That was all she needed.

"I need to grow up and get my life together. I'll get a job. Maybe in the hospital."

"That's where you grow up fast."

"I'll speak to my father."

"Your father?"

"Yes. He works there. He's a cardiologist."

Eric laughed. "I know. But if you want to grow up fast, speak to your mother. You'll grow up faster in the ER."

"My mother may not want me there."

"Of course not. Her plate is full. I've never seen anyone busier. But if you're serious, and if you want to make a difference, that's where you should go."

"Why aren't you there, then?"

"I'm not good enough yet. I'll go when I get better. I can't wait to work with your mother. There's nobody like her."

Taylor grimaced. "I never thought I'd date my mother's fan."

Eric laughed. "You'll be OK. She'll take good care of you."

54

The next day Emma and Sal were working through charts in Emma's office. Her coffee got cold, Sal's Coke got warm, but they still weren't getting anywhere.

"The broken hip looks legit. Nothing weird there," Emma said. "Let's move on to the second case."

"The hypoglycemia?"

"Yes. The labs are back. The C-peptide is low."

"Yep. That means she received insulin. There's no order for it," Sal said.

"How about the order for the patient next door?"

Sal checked. "Thirty units of regular insulin. Dr. Crump's order."

"Who took it out? And when?"

"George did. At 11:55."

"Did he administer it?"

"Yes. He gave it at 12:48."

"George did?"

"Yes."

"It's a long time from 11:55 to 12:48."

"It sure is. What did he do with that vial for almost an hour? Carried it in his pocket? Left it on the counter? Why?" Sal wondered.

"Something happened. He got sucked into something else."

"That's why his glucose was unchanged an hour later. He had just received the insulin; it didn't have time to work." Sal went back to the computer.

"What are you looking at?"

"I'm checking who wasted the rest of it. He took out a 100 units vial. He gave 30 units. He's supposed to discard the rest. With a witness." He went through screen after screen, his nimble fingers falling over the keyboard like hail. "I can't find documentation of it being discarded."

"Seventy units of insulin just disappeared?"

"It looks like it."

"Strange."

"Yes. When did the woman die?"

Emma checked. "The code was terminated at 2:03."

"That fits. If she got the insulin IV, she'd get hypo-glycemic in minutes."

Emma wrote herself a note. *Ask George.*

"Next case is my back pain. Carlos got the meds for him."

Sal checked. "He did. At 2:31."

"Were they even given? By whom?"

"He gave them at 2:45."

"He said he left them on the counter."

Sal shrugged. "That's not what the computer says."

"What identifier do they use to record giving meds?"

"They can use their ID card and a PIN. Or a fingerprint."

"Same with discarding meds?"

"Yes."

Weird. Carlos said he didn't give the meds. And he couldn't have. At 2:45 we were working on the arrhythmia in Room 2.

"I'll have to speak to Carlos."

"You have a lot of talking to do." Sal looked at his watch.

"Something still bugs me about the first case," Emma said. "Can you have another look?"

Sal looked at the orders. He confirmed the meds.

"It looks OK. Brenda got her meds at 3:35. She gave her the Toradol and the morphine at 3:47..."

"Morphine?"

"Yes. Morphine, 4 milligrams. As prescribed."

"But..." Emma went back to the chart. "The tox report says she was positive for fentanyl."

"Fentanyl?"

They looked at each other. They remembered February.

The time of many deaths. The time of fentanyl.

55

That evening, Emma drove home thinking about February. That had been the worst month of her life. She hoped the fentanyl was just a coincidence.

She got home. Guinness was waiting.

"How was your day?" Emma dropped her bag on Victor's chair.

One tail thump.

"OK? Just OK?"

"What did you expect? I was locked in the house the whole day. How was your day?"

"It sucked. But I made a little progress. I figured out the insulin. I also know that Carlos couldn't give those meds..."

Guinness left.

"That's rude. You don't just leave in the middle of a conversation!"

She went to choose a wine. The best part of her day was about to begin.

The Rioja? A little sharp on an empty stomach. The

Californian Oaked Chardonnay? She hated oak. She didn't think much about Chardonnays either.

That's got to be a gift from a beer lover.

She found a new St. Emilion. Chateay Puy Blanquet St. Emilion Grand Cru 2012. *That should be interesting.* She pulled out the cork with a satisfying pop and filled a crystal glass. *Everything tastes better in crystal. Even water. It gives you a feeling of luxury and decadence.* She lifted the glass, looking through it into the light. A little transparent for a Bordeaux. Glowing red. Like a pinot noir. She sniffed it. Hints of fennel and black raspberry. It smelled tart. She tasted it. Quite an edge for a Bordeaux. Not smooth. Her mouth puckered. *It's sour. Decadent, my ass.*

Guinness dropped the leash at Emma's feet and stared, thumping her tail.

"What are you saying?"

"Let's go for a walk."

"Seriously! Now?"

"Yep. Right now." Guinness barked twice and headed to the door.

"I guess it's urgent." Emma sat down the glass. "Let me get changed at least!"

"Not necessary." Guinness said, dancing in front of the door.

I wanted a dog. It's almost as bad as being married! Not quite as bad as having children, though. She glanced at Taylor's closed door.

"Let me have a glass of wine at least."

Guinness disagreed.

The phone rang.

Amber?

Victor's wife was no longer a rival. She wasn't exactly a

friend, but she was Taylor's stepmother. And, deep in her heart, Emma felt sorry for her.

"Hi Amber."

"I'm sorry to bother you."

"No bother. What's up?"

Long pause. "You got a minute?"

"Sure. I'm just walking the dog."

"Can we meet?"

"Now?"

"If possible."

It's late, it's dark, and I have a dog that needs walking. The marina down the road has a terrace and margaritas. And they love dogs.

"Dizzy Alligator?"

"I'll be there in fifteen."

I love kids.
        Pretty kids. Nice kids. Normal kids.
        Not this. This is not a kid.

This is thirty pounds of human flesh kept alive by devices. Peg tube, tracheostomy, ventilator. He's got contractures everywhere. He's so folded he'd fit in my carry on. Not that I'd want to take him anywhere.

I check his chart. Evan. He's twelve. He can't see, he can't talk, he can't eat, he can't breathe.

What's the point of being alive? If you call this alive. He doesn't know he's alive. He can't think.

Can he feel? Let's find out.

I stick a #18 needle in his heel.

He pulls away and tries to scream. He can't. He snorts.

He feels pain. That sucks. I wouldn't have my dog live like this! Any dog! And he's human, if only in name.

I look around. They're all busy.

I turn off the alarms and I detach his tracheostomy from the vent. I cover it with my palm, pretending I'm cleaning it. I wait for the heart to stop.

It takes forever.

I reconnect the vent and leave.

Bye-bye, Evan. If they ask, tell them Carlos sent you!

57

E mma threw a jacket over her scrubs and headed to the Dizzy Alligator to meet Amber. Guinness stopped by the hydrants to check her mail.

What the hell is this about? It's got to be about Victor. I hope it's not bad. He may be a pain, but he's my best friend.

Emma sat at the corner table. Guinness lay at her feet. Emma watched the couple next door gazing at the moon shimmering across the water. Guinness watched them eat their nachos.

It's a full moon. It's going to be another fun night in the ED.

The waiter, old and shriveled under his red baseball cap, stopped by to take their order.

"Two margaritas and a water dish."

Guinness barked.

"What?"

Guinness stared at the neighbor's nachos. Her dinner was late. Emma shrugged. "And an order of nachos."

Emma's margarita vanished almost as fast as Guinness's nachos. She grabbed the second glass.

"Hi, Emma."

She sat the glass down.

"Thanks for coming."

"Of course." Emma signaled the waiter for another drink. *Make it two. It looks like a long night.*

"I couldn't think of anybody else," Amber sighed.

Emma smiled. Thinking had never been Amber's strong point.

"It's about Victor. Things aren't going well at home. He works all the time. He barely sees the kids. They spend more time with the babysitter than they do with him."

Emma nodded.

"He's so distant. We used to do foolish little things, like dancing in the kitchen after the kids went to sleep. Not anymore. Now, it's just work, sleep, and more work."

"I'm sorry," Emma lied. *You stole my husband. Now you're stuck with him.*

"Thank you. You're generous."

Not really.

"You must be wondering why I'm telling you this." Amber wiped her dry eyes. "You know him. You're his friend. He'll listen to you. Something is happening. He's in trouble. Financially? Professionally? I've even wondered if he's doing drugs."

Emma shivered.

"Or if he found somebody else."

That day in the cafeteria, he hinted at getting back together. I'd rather have a root canal.

"That's awful, Amber. Maybe he's just overwhelmed. Did you talk to him?"

"I tried. I prepared a nice dinner. I got wine and candles. Even some nice lingerie—you know what I mean... He didn't come home that night. He said he had to switch call with a colleague."

My ex-husband's wife complaining to me that he's not interested in her. You can't make this shit up.

"Have you thought about counseling? Lots of couples swear by it."

"Maybe... He's so remote... I wondered..." She gave Emma a speculative look. "Would you talk to him?"

"Me?"

"He respects you. He cares about your opinion."

Not so much. He left me for you, remember? But what's the point? That was long ago.

"What would you like me to tell him, Amber?"

"Tell him how hard it is for a woman to be excluded from her man's life. I need him. The girls need him. He needs to reorder his priorities."

"I don't know, Amber. This is very personal. He'll think that I'm intruding. And he would be right. You need to talk to him."

Tears shimmered down Amber's moonlit face. "Please, Emma! You have to help me! There's nobody else I can ask."

Emma wished she could say no. But she couldn't. *I asked for her help last time Taylor disappeared. It's my turn now.* She drained the melted margarita and grimaced. It had plenty of sugar but not much alcohol. She sighed.

"I'll see what I can do."

Amber's face lit up. "Thank you, Emma. I knew I could count on you."

Shoulders slumped, head down, Emma walked home. She felt trapped. She hated doing this, but she had promised.

"Crap."

Guinness cocked her head.

"She conned you into this? I thought you were the smart one."

"Don't even go there!" Emma said.

Guinness wagged her tail.

"Hey, get over it! At least he's her problem now."

58

It was Taylor's first day on the job. Her heart was pumping and she was sick to her stomach. She wished she hadn't been so adamant about getting a job. *In the ER, of all places. What was I thinking?* She had to choose between nursing assistant and environmental worker. Cleaning was so not her thing! She went for nursing assistant. She couldn't figure out how to tell her mother, so she didn't. And today was the day.

She said good-bye to Guinness and climbed into Eric's car. He dropped her off at the ER entrance. She snuck in, hoping to miss her mother.

They paired her with Amy for orientation. Amy had worked there for years, so she knew the ropes. She taught Taylor how to check vital signs. She told her which thermometer went in the mouth, and which at the other end. She showed her how to stock cupboards and how to draw blood. By noon, Taylor's head was spinning.

By far the hardest thing was dealing with patients and families. They always had questions.

"You need to speak to the doctor," Amy said.

"When is he coming?"

"In a few minutes."

"We've been here for an hour."

"He'll come soon. It's busy today. The sicker patients get seen first."

"Never say anything else, even if you know the doctor won't see them for hours," Amy told her afterwards. "And always listen to your nurses. If you have their back, they'll have yours. Try to do what's needed before they even ask. Get a urine. Check vitals. You'll make a lot of friends. Don't worry about the doctors. Your go-to is your nurse."

"I thought the doctors run the show."

"Nah, the nurses just let them think so. The nurses run the show. The doctors come and go. Don't worry about them. Except for Dr. Steele. Be careful with her."

"Why?"

"She's the ED director. She makes things happen when nobody else can."

"How come?"

"She's a witch."

Taylor laughed.

"Really. She reads minds. It's like a seventh sense."

"Sixth," Taylor said.

"Whatever. Don't lie. If you forgot something, just tell her. If you lie, she'll know it. It's not worth it."

You got that one right. It's not worth it.

A handsome doctor in a navy suits stopped by.

"Amy, I need help with a pelvic."

"Yes, Dr. Crump. This is Taylor. She'll be working with us."

"Welcome, Taylor. The ER is a fun place to work. When it doesn't suck."

"Good to know."

He glanced at her belly. "Pregnant?"

"Yes."

"How far?"

"Twenty weeks."

"Congratulations. Amy will show you the ropes. She'll teach you well."

"Yes, Dr. Crump. What room?"

"Room 14."

Setting up the pelvic was the complicated process of transforming the room into a torture chamber complete with stirrups, lights, and tubes. Taylor shivered. She still hadn't seen an OB.

No wonder the patient is distraught.

"I'm sorry, but you may lose this pregnancy. It's too early to tell."

The young woman burst into sobs. Dr. Crump touched her shoulder.

"Is this your first pregnancy?"

"My second."

"You have a baby at home?"

The woman sobbed harder. "I lost that pregnancy at six months."

"I'm sorry."

Taylor was too. She felt the woman's pain as if it was her own.

"We'll know more after the ultrasound," Dr. Crump said.

He opened the door for her. They walked into Emma.

"Taylor?"

Taylor blushed.

"You've already met?" Dr. Crump asked.

"A while ago. Taylor is my daughter."

Dr. Crump looked from one to the other. He glanced at Taylor's belly. "Really?"

"Sometimes I wonder too. But that's what her father told me."

Taylor smiled.

I learned that from Mother. Smile whenever things turn to shit. You'll feel better. Plus, nobody needs to know you're hurting, or they'll hit you even harder.

59

The following morning Emma found a white envelope in her work mailbox. She hoped it wasn't a complaint, or another nastygram from Quality, bashing her performance on the sepsis protocol. She took out the golden-edged invitation.

"North Country University has the pleasure... Dr. Tolpeghin's retirement party... Keynote speaker 5p.m. Cocktails on the lawn 5:30 to 7. Heavy appetizers."

Who?

She read it again. She shrugged and dropped it in the wastebasket. It had to be a mistake. Then she remembered.

It's the Russian. The board member. She said she's a professor! But why invite me? We barely met. I won't know anybody there. I'm probably working anyhow.

She wasn't. That evening was hers to waste as she chose, so she chose to waste it there. She had nothing better to do, after walking Guinness. She put on a forgiving cayenne pepper red dress, matching lipstick, and a pair of non-croc shoes. She glanced in the mirror. The mirror smiled.

She was late, but not late enough. The keynote speech was slow.

"We were incredibly blessed to have Dr. Tolpeghin in our midst. She created an interest in biology that was duly received by our students whose hearts were opened to the miracles of the natural world thanks to her..."

Where do these people learn how to speak? And, more importantly, why?

She looked for the exit. *Back through the crowd, toward the toilets, then I swerve to the parking lot.*

She apologized, slithering back through the crowd, when a hand caught her arm.

"I'm so glad I found you! I looked everywhere!"

Boris?

Looking nothing like a jack-o'-lantern, Boris stole the show in his charcoal suit. His unruly silver blond hair set off his tan; his laughing blue eyes caressed her. In a strange Russian greeting, he kissed her cheeks three times. His skin smelled green and expensive, like French cologne spilled in a deep wood.

"Vera will be delighted to see you," he said, taking her hand and dragging her through the crowd.

Sitting on the podium in a red hat that would put Queen Elizabeth to shame, Vera yawned. Boris waved. Vera saw them and smiled. She winked, signaling them to wait.

The keynote speaker handed her the microphone. Applause spread through the crowd like wildfire.

"Thank you all for being here. It was a privilege to work with you. Let's fight climate change and save the environment. It's the only one we have."

She stepped off the podium to a thunderous ovation.

"That's it?" Boris asked.

"That's all I had to say. I don't need half an hour to say it."

Emma laughed. Vera hugged her.

"Welcome. I'm glad you came. I didn't think you would, but Boris said it was worth a try."

"It's always worth a try for something you care about, Vera. Isn't that what you taught me?"

"Thank you for inviting me," Emma said.

"My pleasure," Boris answered. "Don't worry, Vera, I'll take care of her. You go deal with your boring crap."

"Be good," Vera said.

"Where's the fun in that?" Boris asked.

"Then at least be smart," she laughed.

"Come. I'll take you to the cocktails," Boris said.

Emma hesitated. "Are you sure..."

He laughed. "It's OK, Dr. Steele. Relax. I'm no longer your patient. You're not responsible for me. How about having fun for a change?"

Fun? I guess... She wished she could remember how.

Boris did. He ordered for her. In tune with Vera's speech, they had cocktails she'd never heard of, like "Penguin Melter" and "Polar Heatwave" and "Antarctic Beach." He drank club soda with lime, enjoying her pleasure. He made her laugh, he made her think, and he made her feel like a woman worth looking at. Emma was bewitched.

He's the most exciting man I ever met since Victor. Scratch that. He's the most exciting man I've ever met.

The evening was magical and short.

"I'll drive you home," Boris said.

"Thanks, but I drove here."

"That was before the cocktails. I'll drive you home. I'll bring you back to get your car tomorrow morning."

"I work at seven."

"I get up at five."

Emma hesitated.

"Emma, I'll call you a taxi if you want. I'm not looking for sex. Maybe later. Right now, I'm looking for friendship, companionship, and a good laugh. More than anything, I'm looking to keep you safe. You matter to me."

He drove her home. They talked. She told him about her job, about her life, about how poorly she was doing at everything. He listened. He told her about sleeping on tatami mats in Japan, about centenary turtles having sex in the Galapagos, about the Folex—fake Rolex—he had bought in Alexandria.

Guinness came to meet them at the door. She stared at him with her amber eyes, sniffing every inch of his pants. He laughed and talked to her in Russian. Guinness smiled.

"What did you tell her?" Emma asked.

"A secret," he said, scratching the dog behind her ears. "She'll tell you if she wants to."

They sat on the green leather sofa. They talked. He was an artist, working in mixed media. Never married. He hadn't found the right girl until now. His aunt was his godmother and his only family. He played chess.

He asked about her. She told him she had a daughter. And an ex-husband. And a job.

"And? Tell me more about you."

"That's it," she said.

He hugged her. "Let's go to bed."

She blushed. He laughed. "Don't worry. I'll just hold you."

She took him to her bed. He held her. He told her she was wonderful. She laughed.

He didn't. "The one thing I'd like to do is to show you

how beautiful you are. You're smart. You're funny. You're wonderful."

Emma laughed.

"I'm serious. Beauty is in the soul, not in the fashion magazines. Look at the most beautiful women ever. Rubens's. Rembrandt's. Renoir's. Look at the freaking Mona Lisa. Not a single one of them is less than a size 12. You need to put on a few pounds to fit in."

Emma chuckled, but she stopped worrying about her body.

They slept embraced. For the first time, she felt at peace with who she was. She wasn't young, she wasn't thin, but she was OK.

It's not only what you do. It's also who you are. And I'm not so bad!

She couldn't wait for their date next week.

60

Next day in the ER, Taylor was having a bad shift. She wasn't feeling well. Her eyes burned with tears. She'd already stuck the patient in Room 10, again and again. No luck. The patient, a lovely old lady, didn't complain, but her family was giving her rotten looks. She told Faith. Faith sent her back to try again.

Taylor gathered her tubes but couldn't bring herself to go in. She stared at the door, tears streaming down her cheeks. Carlos touched her shoulder.

"What's up?" he asked.

"I can't get the labs."

"Go tell your nurse."

"I did. She told me to try again. 'It's the only way to learn,' she said. But I tried three times already."

"Why don't you send this urine for me, then? I'll get the blood for you. Nobody needs to know."

"Thank you, Carlos."

Taylor sent the urine. She returned just as Carlos brought out the labs.

"Thanks, Carlos!" Taylor hugged him.

"Isn't that cute!" Faith said.

Carlos frowned and left without a word. Faith stared at Taylor's belly.

"Is it his?"

"What?" Taylor asked

Faith's chin pointed to her pregnant belly.

"Of course not," Taylor said.

"Whose is it then?"

Taylor's blood rose to her cheeks.

"None of your business. These are your labs." She walked away to chill. Fortunately, it was time for her lunch.

Eric was right. In the ER you grow up fast.

She was learning to control her temper. She couldn't help but notice that some tragedies were worse than her smeared mascara or somebody's snide remark. She was learning about real life. It wasn't always fun, but it was enlightening.

By the end of her break she had chilled. She walked back just as the speakers sputtered: "Code 99, ER, Room 10."

That's my room. The patient that I couldn't get blood from. She rushed to Room 10, now awash with scrubs, and squeezed in.

Faith was performing CPR. Dr. Crump was running the code. The family stared in horror. The lovely smiling lady was now dead.

Nothing helped. Dr. Crump called the code. Taylor didn't understand.

"What happened?" she asked Faith.

Faith's limpid blue eyes didn't blink.

"She died."

"Why?"

"Her day has come." Faith smiled. "Why don't you ask your friend Carlos?"

I'll ask Mother.

That evening she waited for her mother to came home. She watched her drop her bag and pet Guinness. She watched her pour her wine. Her hands, cracked from too much washing, shook from too much coffee. Her bloodshot eyes, dried by the air-conditioning, had deep dark circles.

For the first time ever, Taylor felt sorry for her mother. *She's so tired she's gray. She's vulnerable. She's actually mortal.* She wished she hadn't seen that. It made her feel responsible for her mother, and she didn't need that. It was hard enough to be responsible for herself.

She told her the story.

"Faith told me to ask Carlos."

"How long had it been since Carlos was in the room?"

"Half an hour maybe?"

"Did he give her anything?"

"No. He just got the bloods."

"How did he get them?"

"From the vein?"

"Did she have an IV?"

"Yes. But I can't use that. I had to stick her again to get the blood."

"You can't, but nurses can. They get blood from the IV, then they flush it, so that it doesn't clot. Was the family there?"

"Yes."

"Even when Carlos went in?"

"I don't know."

Emma sipped on her wine.

"What do you think?" Taylor asks.

"I think Carlos is in major trouble."

"Why?"

"That's exactly the question. Why? Why is somebody trying to sink Carlos? And who?"

"It's Ben," Taylor said.

"Why Ben?"

"I heard him talk to Mike the other day."

"What did he say?"

"He said Carlos is back with his old friends. He thinks he's stealing drugs."

"What did Mike say?"

"He asked for proof."

"And?"

"Ben said he'll get it. Soon."

61

Emma lay awake that night, thinking about it. Could Taylor be right? Was Ben behind the string of deaths, trying to sink Carlos? Hard to believe. She ran the day's events through her head once more.

Emma was in her office when they called the code. She was struggling to make sense of the latest death. A kid. Vent-dependent, brought in for a fever, looking stable. Carlos's patient. Chest X-ray looked like pneumonia. Vitals were fine. Then he just died. Before the X-ray got read.

Why? No idea. This has got to be another one in that string. Except for the age, everything else fits. Looking OK, dead half an hour later for no reason.

"Code 99, Emergency Department, Room 10."

Emma had grabbed her stethoscope and ran. Room 10 was a sea of scrubs, working feverishly. Kurt ran the code. Emma met his haggard eyes.

"Can I help?"

"Another epi please. Continue CPR." He turned to Emma. "Can you look at the heart?"

Emma brought in the ultrasound machine. The translucent algae-green gel splashed on the probe with a liquid sound. She held up the probe, waiting for a break.

"Check for a pulse," Kurt said. In a smooth move, Faith stepped back from doing CPR, making room for Amy to step forward. Kurt felt the neck for a pulse. All eyes were on the ultrasound screen. Emma placed the probe to the left of the sternum, between the second and third ribs. She pushed it down hard, to make contact. The heart, a pear-shaped dark shadow, materialized on the screen. No movement but the valves, waving, carried by the blood. No contraction.

"We'll call this code," Kurt said, wiping his face with his sleeve. He looked at Emma. "This is ridiculous."

Emma nodded.

She returned to her office to check the chart. Somebody knocked at the half open door.

"Come in."

Sal came in.

"Have a seat. Problem?"

"I found this in Room 10," he said, showing her a vial.

Emma reached for it. He pulled it back.

"Gloves."

She gloved. "Propofol. 200 mg. Empty."

"Yes. I was wasting the meds in the RSI kit when I found this on the counter. It wasn't in the kit. That one was still there. Untouched."

"Dr. Crump didn't order anything for this patient."

"Correct."

"Could it be left in the room from the previous patient?"

"Unlikely. The room had just been through a terminal clean after an infectious patient."

"Weird."

"It gets worse. The serial number identifies this vial as

part of an RSI kit Carlos took out last week. He recorded wasting it."

Carlos.

"That's enough to kill that tiny old woman."

"If she got it."

"Yes, if she got it."

"The labs will tell. Either way, Carlos is in trouble."

"Major trouble."

"What next?"

"I'll tell Mike and the pharmacy director. They'll take it from there. I just thought you'd want to know."

"Thanks, Sal."

Carlos? Killing all these people? Not likely.

She went back to her cases.

The door opened wide. Kurt stepped in looking like he'd slept in his clothes, his usual spunk gone. Emma offered him a chair and chocolate.

"I wish it was wine."

"Me too. Who the hell is doing this? Why? And how?"

"Kurt, you're sure you didn't give her anything?"

"Come on, Emma!"

"Sorry, I have to ask."

"Not even Tylenol."

"Sal found an empty vial of propofol in the room."

"I didn't order propofol. I didn't order anything, for fuck's sake!"

"OK. I guess we'll find out."

"Sorry, Emma. I'm just tired and frustrated. I'm sure you are too." He cleared his voice.

"Your daughter...I didn't know she was pregnant."

"Yep. The joys of parenthood."

"How old is she?"

"Eighteen."

"Is she...what is she going to do with the baby?"

"Good question. I don't think she knows. It's been a rocky ride."

Kurt stood. "I'd better head home; I'm late already. Sheila won't like it." He stopped with his hand on the door-knob. "You know, Emma..." He shifted his weight from one leg to the other. "Sheila and I, we're looking at adopting. In case...if Taylor is considering it, we'd welcome not only the baby but Taylor too. Sheila would be overjoyed."

"I'll tell Taylor. I'll tell her to speak to you if she thinks that's something she may consider."

"Thanks, Emma."

Should I tell him that the baby's father is... No. That's up to Taylor.

62

M ike's office was packed the next morning. They held an emergency meeting. Nobody was happy. The voices were high, the tempers short, and the oxygen mostly gone. Emma squeezed a seat between Sal and Brenda.

"The latest event was yesterday. Another patient, MR 0897654454, here for a syncope, waiting for her workup to be completed, arrested suddenly and with no explanation and was unable to be resuscitated." Mike glanced around to make sure they were all paying attention.

Emma uncrossed her legs and crossed them the other way. *I hate medicalese! Why can't we speak like normal people? "Wasn't able to be resuscitated." We weren't able to resuscitate her. That's just like "the patient failed the treatment" bullshit. It's the treatment that failed the patient.*

"This has to stop. We have lost more patients in the last few weeks than in a whole quarter of last year. The Quality team started an investigation. The state will come after us, sooner rather than later, to look into this increased mortality. We can't afford to wait and see what happens. We have to be proactive. We have to stop this."

Proactive my ass! Proactive meant stopping it before it started. If anything, this is post-active.

"I agree," Gus said. "We should have done something long ago."

"What are you saying, Mike?" Judy asked.

"I think we should put Carlos on a leave of absence while we're looking into things."

"Carlos? Why Carlos?"

"Carlos was involved with a bunch of these deaths. He was the primary nurse of four of them. He was also involved with the care of a few of the others," Mike said.

"That in itself doesn't mean anything," Emma said. "So was I. So was Sal."

Sal frowned.

"Come on, Sal, you know what I mean. There's no evidence against Carlos."

"Actually, there is. He was the one who gave the meds to that back-pain patient of yours who died. Then he said he didn't. But it's in the computer. He signed for them."

"That's exactly what worries me. I know he didn't. He was with me in another room. We were working on an arrhythmia. He couldn't be in two places at the same time."

Mike shrugged. "It only takes a minute to leave the room and give the meds. Nobody would even notice."

"And log into the computer to sign that you did? Then deny it? It makes no sense."

"It may not make sense to you, but it's going to make a lot of sense to the police. Then there's the RSI kit."

"What RSI kit?" Gus asked.

"Sal, can you explain?"

"One of Carlos's patients got intubated a few days ago. Carlos took out an RSI kit. They used a couple of meds, not all of them. Carlos recorded discarding the rest. There was no witness. Then, yesterday, a patient coded. The empty vial of propofol found at her bedside belonged to that discarded RSI kit.

"That's bad," Gus said. "That's awful."

"Still, it doesn't explain everything. Some of the incidents didn't involve Carlos."

"That we know of," Mike said. "Not yet. By the way, remember that patient with the agitated daughter, the pneumonia in Room 15? Your patient?"

"Yes."

"George was your nurse."

"Yes."

"George went on break. Carlos covered for him. When George came back, she was dead."

"George and Carlos room together," Judy said.

"What are you saying?" Emma asked.

"Nothing. Just thinking out loud."

"Then this last patient. The one with the propofol vial. It was Faith's patient, but Carlos went to draw blood. When Faith went back, she was dead."

"Death seems to be following Carlos," Gus said. "If he's not guilty, he sure is unlucky."

"What if somebody is framing Carlos?" Emma asked. "Some cases he's not involved with. Some things make no sense. First, why would he do this?"

"Why would anybody do this?" Judy asked.

"Because they're nuts," Mike answered.

"But why sign that you gave meds to a patient you're trying to kill? Shouldn't he pretend he never did? That makes no sense."

"Maybe he forgot and did it by reflex," Mike said.

"This is complicated. It doesn't look like we can clarify it today," Gus said, "We'll work on it. But in the meantime, we have to do everything we can to protect our patients. I say Carlos is out."

"What if it's not him? What if this continues?" Emma said.

Gus glowered at her.

"What do you want to do, Emma?"

"We should call the police. Have them look into things."

"Absolutely not! If somebody leaks the news, we're cooked! Nobody will come here any longer for fear of being killed! We'll go bankrupt. We have to clarify this first."

"We'll be even more cooked if we watch people dying and don't do anything," Emma said.

"That's precisely why we are putting Carlos on a leave of absence," Gus said.

"What if it's not him? What if it's somebody framing him? And they're still here?"

Mike shrugged. "If they're framing him and he's gone, maybe they'll stop the killings."

Emma's jaw fell. "Really? Is this the best we can do?"

"I'm afraid so. In the circumstances," Gus said. He stood. "I'm sorry, but I have another meeting. We'll put Carlos on a leave of absence and we'll see how this goes."

Emma opened her mouth to say something, but Sal touched her elbow.

"They've made up their minds," he whispered. "There's no point in pushing it. You'll just make enemies."

He's right. I guess I'll have to continue to work on it myself. At least now I know what I'm looking for.

Emma ran into Faith on her way to her car. Faith smiled. Emma wanted to stop, but she couldn't. Something inside her said no. She felt Faith's eyes burning into her back. Something stirred in the pit of her stomach. She shivered.

I t worked. I can't believe it! It was less than twelve bucks on Amazon. It doesn't look like much. A piece of green plastic, looking like a luggage scale. It fits in my scrubs pocket.

I wait until she goes to sew a laceration. She always leaves her coat on the chair, so she doesn't get blood on it. Her ID hangs from the chest pocket.

I snatch it as I pass by, and I head to the bathroom.

I get my RFID reader, and aim it at her ID. I press READ.

It beeps.

I get a blank card and aim the RFID reader at it. I press WRITE.

It beeps. It worked.

That's it!

I return her ID. She'll never know I took it.

I wave my new card over the sign-in reader to make sure it works.

It asks for the PIN.

I have it. I got it last week. She was too preoccupied with that sick patient to see me staring at her hands.

I type it in. It works.

I'm Dr. Steele now. I can look up charts, put in orders, document, whatever. Under her signature.

Dr. Angel Steele. Sounds good!

When she got home that evening, Emma checked out the wine rack. She looked for something to warm her inside, to clean her from the day's misery, sadness, and fear. Something unusual caught her eye: Renmano Chairman Selection Shiraz 2017. The bottle was dark green, the label white with a galloping golden horse. That gave her pause. *What does the horse have to do with anything? I hope it's not the flavor! I thought oak and leather were bad.* She shrugged, opened it, poured a glass, and sat on the sofa.

Dark as ink, the wine had a nose of blackberries and plum, with a touch of honey and a hint of pepper. No horse. She took a sip. The wine was full bodied, "corposo" as Italians say, and sensual. She felt its warmth spreading through her. She sighed.

Guinness laid her head on Emma's knees. She rolled belly up, demanding to be scratched.

"I thought you Germans were aloof and dignified." Emma set down her glass to scratch her armpit. Guinness moaned with pleasure.

"What do you think about all this? I think somebody is framing Carlos. He isn't stupid. He wouldn't leave that kind of trail. Somebody's trying to sink him. But why?"

Guinness rolled, offering the other armpit.

"The obvious answer is Faith. They were together, they fell apart, she hates him. But she's a great girl. I'm biased, of course. How could I not be? She saved my life. But she really is patient and caring, especially to the elderly. She'd never do something like this! Carlos has other enemies. Ben got demoted because of Carlos. He almost got fired. Faith said that's just the tail end of the story. There's a lot of bad blood between them. Ben said Carlos is stealing drugs. Was that the propofol vial Sal found? Is there more coming? And what happened to the rest of the RSI kit that vial came from?"

Guinness had no suggestions. She rolled back on her other side.

Emma shook her head. "I'm getting nowhere. I need to speak to him. Let's go."

The red car swallowed the empty roads. George's windows glowed orange in the night.

Emma rang the doorbell. George opened the door, holding a beer.

"Long time no see, stranger. Come in. Beer?"

"No, thanks." Emma shivered looking at the can in his hand. "I'm a wine person."

"Sorry, but I don't..."

"Good. I'm driving anyhow. Is Carlos home?"

"Nope. He came back from work and said they put him on leave. He drove out like a bat out of hell. Said he's going back to New Hampshire to clear his head."

"I see."

"They think he's got something to do with all these deaths, but I don't think so. He's not a killer."

"I agree. But then who is?" Emma asked.

"His girlfriend?"

"I don't think so. She's a nice girl."

"She's not nice. She's disturbed. There's something seriously wrong with her."

"What makes you say that?"

"I've seen her. She's dark inside. Those glass-blue eyes are creepy. They give me the chills."

"I don't think so, George. Just because Carlos is your friend..."

"Listen, Emma. You know me better than that. That girl is trouble."

Emma shrugged. "I'll go now."

"Emma, watch your back. I have a bad feeling."

"What feeling?"

"Something's about to happen."

"Bad things happened already. Too many."

"I know. I have a feeling something bad is going to happen to you."

Emma shuddered. She turned up the heat in the car. She was still shivering when she got home.

Boris was waiting in the driveway.

"I couldn't wait until next week."

Her heart sang.

65

Carlos drove for hours and hours that night. He put mile after mile of dark wet road behind him. His shoulders hurt and his neck was stiff from leaning forward, trying to see beyond his lights. His tired eyes burned from the glare. He was far enough to stop and take a break, but there was nothing. Nothing but the never-ending wet road, the rain, and the forest.

Drunk with rage, he had left on a whim. He couldn't think about anything else to do. He was humiliated and angry.

And guilty.

They called him for an urgent meeting in Mike's office. They were all there: Mike, the VPM, the union representative, the hospital lawyer. They ganged up on him.

They asked about the meds for the back pain.

"I left them on the counter."

"You gave them. There's your signature," Mike said.

"I didn't."

"You signed that you did."

"I didn't."

They didn't believe him.

They asked about the woman in Room 15.

"You covered George's break. How was she?"

That's when Brenda came to me. I never made it there.

"She was fine," he lied.

They asked about Taylor's patient in Room 10.

"Yes, I got the blood."

"What did you give her?"

"Nothing. She wasn't my patient."

"Then why did you get the blood?"

"Taylor needed help."

"How about the propofol?" Mike asked.

What?

"You left the empty vial in the room."

"I didn't leave any vial in the room."

"You did. We checked. It's the propofol from the intubation kit you charted as discarded."

Carlos heard his blood boil, and his brain darkened with fury. Mike was Ben's friend. *That's why he hates me. That's why he blames me.*

But Carlos had indeed charted that stolen RSI kit as discarded. He'd hoped it was gone for good. It wasn't. The propofol had come back to haunt him. *I'm fucked.*

"Don't answer any questions you're not sure about," the union rep intervened. "Even better, don't answer any more questions at all. You need a lawyer."

"I'm here," the hospital lawyer said.

"You're not his lawyer. He needs his own."

Carlos agreed. He didn't need to dig himself any deeper. Security escorted him out, just as Ben was coming in to work. Ben grinned like he'd won the lottery. Carlos ached to punch him in the face. It took all his self-control to refrain.

The smirk on his face! He couldn't wait to go and tell them. As if the whole ER didn't already know.

A burning flash of lightning split the sky. A deafening roll of thunder followed a second later, bringing him back to the present. The rain, falling like a wall of water. The car, skidding on the slick road. A truck's high beams blinded him. He slowed down.

I wish I hadn't left.

Faith and Ben were going to laugh at him. All the others —Brenda, Mike, even Dr. Steele—they'd think he was guilty. And he was. He was guilty of one thing. He had lied about discarding the kit. He had nothing else to be ashamed of. He didn't kill people. He didn't steal drugs. He only tried to do his job and save lives.

Now he was on the run. Ben was laughing. With Faith. His anger made him sick. He opened the window to spit his bile. The rain caressed him with cool fingers. It soothed his forehead and relieved the burn in his eyes.

He couldn't let that happen. He couldn't run away and let them laugh. He had struggled his whole life to become somebody. He couldn't let them steal that. He turned around. *I'm going back. I'll show them. I'll put things right. I'll prove that I'm innocent.*

He drove and drove and drove.

Hours later, he was getting close but he was hurting. He was running out of gas. Another hour or so to go. He rubbed his burning eyes. He saw the lights on the left side of the road. *I almost missed it.*

He turned left.

He didn't see the truck. The road was wet. The night was dark. He wasn't thinking straight.

He slammed the brakes and turned the wheel. The brakes screeched like a dying wild bird. The car swerved, then slid on the slick asphalt. A pole came toward him. He pulled the wheel right, swerved, and slid toward the culvert. He hit it, then flew over it. The car twisted in the air like an Olympic diver. Caught in the blinding headlights, a ghost-like white aspen rushed toward him, upside down. Up again. Upside down.

His head exploded into darkness.

66

Taylor's shift was almost over. She dropped the vials in the transport tube and sighed. She was glad to be done. Her feet hurt. Her back too. She was so hungry she could cry.

Working in the ER wasn't what she expected. She'd learned a lot. Some technical skills, like finger-sticks—sticking needles in people's fingers to check their blood glucose—and measuring vital signs. She learned where to find weird things like the anoscope, for looking into people's nether side, and the Magill forceps, for removing foreign bodies from tight places. She learned about the ER culture. ER people were not like the others. Something about working here made them into a team. Some were nice, some less so, but they were all intense, dedicated, and funny.

Getting exposed to the never-ending human tragedy and the occasional comedy had helped shift her focus beyond herself. An only child, then a deserted child when her father left, she got too much attention. She figured out she was the center of the universe.

Nope. She wasn't sure the universe had a center, but if it

did, she wasn't it. Maybe her mother. People orbited around her mother like planets on a gravitational pull. Taylor's feelings about her mother had changed after she started working in the ER. Her mother had a peculiar way of interacting with people. They were attracted to her like cats to a sun patch. It was like wherever she was, it was warmer.

Taylor got her bag and headed out. The door opened and she walked into Dr. Crump. She apologized. He smiled.

"Hi Taylor."

"Hello."

"Done for the day?"

"Yes, thank God."

He laughed. "That's what we all say."

They walked out the door. The sky had broken into sheets of rain. Taylor stopped under the awning to get her phone.

"You need a ride?"

"I...I was calling Eric, my boyfriend, to pick me up."

"I'll take you. No bother, I live that way anyhow. You're living with your mother, right?"

"Yes."

"Let's go. Even better, wait here. I'll get the car."

Taylor felt uncomfortable. Why would he give her a ride? She was just a nursing assistant. He was a doctor. And married. Was it...No, he didn't give off that sort of vibe. He was handsome and all, but she was over older men. She had Eric.

His blue Audi arrived and she climbed in. Next to his beautiful dark suit, her scrubs looked out-of-place. She wished she'd waited another five minutes so she wouldn't have to ride with him. She sat up straight, her bag on her knees, trying to cover her bulging belly.

"How's it going? How do you like the ER?"

"It's like no other place. It's fascinating, scary, and exhilarating, all at the same time. Awful and disgusting, at times."

He laughed. "I couldn't say it better myself. The fact that your mother works there must make it harder."

"I haven't worked with her. Not yet."

"You probably won't. She'll try to avoid that."

Taylor nodded.

"How are you feeling?" He took a quick glance at her belly.

Taylor blushed. "I'm all right."

"Do you know if it's a boy or a girl?"

"No."

"You like surprises?"

I hate surprises. I can't remember ever having a good surprise. From Dad leaving home to this pregnancy, plus everything about Dick, every surprise I had was a blow across the head. I hate them with a passion. And I hope there won't be any surprises about this kid, though it would be a surprise if there were no surprises.

"Not so much."

He nodded as if he understood.

"When is the baby due?"

"September."

"That's a good month. The weather is still nice, but the heat of the summer is over."

Not like I planned it this way.

"Have you thought about what you'll do?"

Taylor bristled. *That's none of your business.*

"I know it's none of my business." He drove slowly, looking straight ahead. "But I'd like to tell you a story."

May as well. I hope we get home soon.

"My wife, Sheila, and I, we've been married for twenty-three years. We hoped for children. Sheila did. For me, it wasn't that important. We tried everything. No luck. We went to in vitro fertilization. Sheila became pregnant. Unfortunately, she lost the pregnancy. We tried again. She carried that one to twenty-two weeks, then lost it. She was devastated. She became depressed and withdrawn. We tried all sorts of treatments. Nothing worked. Our marriage... our marriage went through some rough patches. I almost lost her." He choked.

"I'm sorry," Taylor mumbled.

"She's better now. We are better now. We're talking adoption."

Taylor looked out the window. *Five more minutes.*

"I saw you're pregnant. You're so young. You have your whole life ahead of you. I don't know if giving up your child for adoption is something you've considered, but I'd love you to meet Sheila. She's wonderful. She'll be a great mother. We'd welcome your baby. We'd welcome you too. You could spend as much time with him as you wanted. We'd be happy to have you both."

"That's... very generous of you."

"Not at all. It would be generous of you."

"I haven't decided what to do. I'm still trying to find my bearings."

"I understand. I just wanted to put it out there. And I'd love it if you could meet Sheila either way. She's a lovely person and an artist."

"What type of art?"

"Pottery. She has a studio in the back yard."

"I've always had an interest in pottery," Taylor said.

"Why don't you stop by, one of these days," he said, pulling in Emma's driveway.

"I just might. Thank you." She climbed out awkwardly, her thickened belly in the way. He gave it a longing look.

"My pleasure. Good luck, Taylor. Stay in touch."

Taylor smiled and nodded.

Behind the window, a shadow moved.

Guinness was watching.

67

Back in the ER for another shift, Emma finished discharging Room 6. Her phone vibrated. A message from Boris. She smiled. Boris was fun to be with and had the best stories. But, more importantly, he made her feel good about herself. *I can use that.*

"Trauma code, Emergency Department, Room 1." The metallic voice cut through the ER noise, stirring a new urgency in everyone but the patients. The scrubs' chaotic movement gathered into a stream flowing to Room 1. Emma grabbed her stethoscope, straightened her achy back, and followed.

"Mine?" she asked Judy.

"Yes."

"What is it?"

"MVA. Male."

"Anything about his injuries?"

"Head and torso. They're still extricating."

"ETA?"

"Fifteen minutes. Longer if they're having trouble."

Time for the full trauma garb—gown, mask, hat, and

booties. She suited in a hurry. Two minutes later, the room was crammed with masked blue people she could barely recognize. *We look like a den of Martians! Thank God for the yellow labels.* She attached the one labeled "ER Doctor" to her gown. She pulled on her gloves as the sirens started.

She checked her equipment: video laryngoscope, #8 endotracheal tube ready, with the hyper-curved metal stylet inside and the air-filled 10cc syringe attached, oxygen ports ready, suction, warm IV fluids, difficult airway cart.

The sirens got louder. Their wails intertwined like those of lovesick cats. Emma went to the ambulance door to meet them and gain an extra minute to listen to the EMTs.

She punched the silver plate door opener with the back of her fist. She stepped in the ambulance bay. The sirens died. The silence fell heavy on her ears, still buzzing with the ruckus.

The ambulance door opened. Roy, the EMT, held a mask over the patient's face, pumping air into his lungs with his blue AMBU bag. Brandon, his partner, performed CPR. The deep chest compressions squeezed blood out of the heart, pushing it to the essential organs. His strained face shone with sweat. He saw her, and his tension softened. His work was almost done. *They're off the hook. Now it's us.*

"Hello, Dr. Steele. MVA. Thirty-five-year-old male. We have a 20 in the right AC. He was tachycardic and hypotensive when we got him. We just lost the pulse. We gave two rounds of epi. No return of spontaneous circulation. He's been in PEA for the last five minutes."

PEA. Pulseless electric activity. It can be anything. Shock? Tension pneumothorax? Cardiac tamponade?

The helping crew came to help take out the stretcher. The long, articulated metal legs dropped to the ground with a clunk. The stretcher rolled to Room 1, Roy and Brandon glued to it like limpets. Emma joined them. She looked at the patient, trying to assess his injuries. It wasn't easy, since he was covered in blood. *No beard. Thin moustache. No movement, other than the two-inch chest wall rise when Brandon lets it recoil. C-collar stabilizing the neck. The gash above his ear isn't bleeding. Of course not. There's no blood pressure. All bleeding stops. Eventually.*

Brenda stabilized his neck. On her count, they moved him to the ER stretcher. The respiratory therapist took over the airway. The mask made obscene farting noises with every squeeze. *It's leaking air. The bagging's no good.*

"No breathing, no pulse," Emma dictated. "Let's expose him and hook him up to our monitors. Continue CPR."

Trauma shears came out of pockets. Bloody clothes vanished, exposing a bruised, fit body. *Abrasions everywhere; a palm-sized bruise over his left chest. That chest is moving funny.*

Leaning over the head of the bed, Emma pried open the eyes. "Pupils 4 mm, equal and reactive to light. Ten-inch laceration to the left parietal region, oozing blood." *Something about him looks familiar.* She wiped the blood off his face.

Carlos.

She took in a sharp breath. She opened her mouth to tell them. She closed it back. *They don't need that added stress. It won't help.*

"Dr. Steele!"

Kayla, the ER clerk, stood in the doorway, her face whiter than snow.

"The police are here. We have an ID."

"Yes. Get me the allergies and medical history please."

"It's..."

"I know." Emma tried to stop her.

"Carlos!"

The room gasped. They stepped forward to see him better.

"Back, everybody! We have a patient to save." Emma's voice cracked like a whip over the room. They stepped back. All but Faith. Faith moved in.

Her blue eyes swallowed her face. She sobbed. She screamed.

"Carlos! What did you do? Why did you do this?" Hands shaking, she touched him, exploring him as if she couldn't see. She bent over him close enough to kiss him.

Emma caught Judy's eye. She nodded to the door. Judy put her arm around Faith's shoulders, guiding her out.

"We need a surgeon," Emma said.

"I paged him. He didn't call back," Kayla answered.

"Page him again. Hold the scanner."

She turned back to Brenda: "What do we have for IV access? Labs?"

"Got a 20 from EMS. Working on a second," Brenda said.

"Good. Getting it would be even better. We need a second line and labs. I need a type and cross. He'll need a transfusion." *If he makes it.*

"Amy, get me the IO drill. How's he bagging?"

"Poorly" the RT said, pulling the face into the mask to improve the seal.

"Try an oral airway and reposition the jaw." She turned to Chris. "Start transfusing."

Still no second line.

"The IO?"

Judy handed it to her.

Emma glanced at Carlos. *Almost six feet, maybe 70 kilos.* She chose the two-inch yellow intraosseous needle and screwed it in the business end of the drill. She cleaned the skin below the knee joint and placed the needle tip at a right angle to the shin. She pushed her weight into the drill, then pulled the trigger.

The drill bit into bone. The bone cracked as the needle broke through.

Emma checked the placement. *Solid.* She took out the stylet, attached a syringe to the IO needle, and sucked in the murky red fluid. *Bone marrow. I'm in.* She flushed it and handed it to Chris.

Amy stepped back. Gina took her place, continuing CPR.

Still nothing. He's as good as dead, but maybe... The chest injury—maybe a tension pneumo? Or cardiac tamponade? Either of those could stop his heart. Worth a try. He can't get any deader. She splashed green phosphorescent gel on the ultrasound probe.

"Stop CPR."

She placed the probe on the chest. Left of the sternum, between the second and the third ribs. She glanced at the screen. A thick black stripe between the probe and the quivering heart. *Tamponade. That black stripe is blood around the heart, squeezing it shut. The only way to save him is to stick a needle in it and drain it. But the surgeon isn't here and the only pericardiocentesis I ever did was on a pig, in the simulation lab. The pig didn't make it. I guess I get to do a real one today. I hope it works out better.*

She cleaned the area below the probe with disinfectant. She donned sterile gloves and took the catheter from Judy. It was a 14, as big as a knitting needle, only meaner. Just looking at it made her sick. Her hands shook. She took a slow, deep breath to steady them. She rested the back of her right hand on his chest. Her left pressed the probe into the skin. The needle went in. Its tip, a bright dot of light, appeared on the screen above the dark stripe. She advanced the needle, watching the white tip progress toward the dark stripe. One more centimeter. She got in.

Like the only star in a dark night sky.

Dark blood flashed in the needle. Emma dropped the probe. She held the catheter in with one hand and pulled out the monster needle with the other.

His blood, dark red and warm, splattered her, covering her glasses. She grabbed the large syringe with her bloody gloved hand. It was so slippery she almost dropped it. She struggled to attach it without displacing the catheter. Blood spurted everywhere, blinding her. By feel alone, she got the syringe attached. It instantly filled.

That's the pressure keeping the heart hostage. They say 25 cc is enough to...

The monitor beeped, dancing with joy. The heart was back.

The room gasped. Emma felt faint.

"We have a pulse. Blood pressure?"

"Checking it."

"Labs?"

"I have them. Sending them now."

"IV access?"

"18 in the left AC, and a 20 in the right AC."

"Surgeon?"

"On his way."

It's a darn long trip. Emma wiped the sweat off her forehead with a bloody sleeve.

"Blood pressure 106/93. Oxygen sat 90%."

"Let's start another unit of blood. Recheck vitals in 3. Sal, let's give TXA."

"He's breathing on his own," the RT said.

Should I intubate? If I do, I get control of the airway but I

may drop his blood pressure. I may even give him a tension pneu-
mothorax.

"Blood pressure 110/90."

It's holding.

"Quick chest X-ray, please. And pelvis. A finger-stick. Let's get ready to intubate."

"What do you want for intubation?" Sal asked.

"Ketamine and Sux, please. Fentanyl first. He's going to need a drip to keep him down when the RSI wears off."

"Propofol?"

"No. That'll drop his blood pressure. Let's do ketamine while we're figuring things out. Then we can switch."

"OK."

She slid the ultrasound probe along his right abdomen, looking for blood. *Big-time black stripe between the liver and the right kidney. He's got blood in his belly.*

"Blood pressure dropping. 85/62."

Damn it. I can't send him to the scanner, and I can't intubate. I don't even know if it's his tamponade reaccumulating or he's bleeding in his belly. Probably both.

"Where's that damn surgeon?"

"The damn surgeon's right here," a tall white coat said, stepping gingerly to avoid the blood pooled on the floor.

"I'm Dr. Roth."

"Hi, Dr. Roth. I'm Emma Steele, and I've never been happier to see a surgeon."

68

C arlos went to the OR. Emma stole a moment to get herself together. She went to the bathroom to clean up. She washed her hands. She rinsed her face with cold water. She breathed. *What a roller coaster. First the trauma code. Then finding out it was Carlos. Dead. Bringing him back, just to see him fall apart again.*

She looked in the mirror. A pale, tired woman looked back. She put on lipstick to improve her morale. It didn't help. She went back to her desk. Judy was waiting.

"Will you speak to Faith? She's the closest thing he's got to family."

Emma wished she could say no. It was too personal. She was close to them both. Besides that, George's suspicion made her weary. She knew Carlos hadn't killed all those people. Somebody else had. *Faith? It can't be. But then who?*

"Sure."

Faith sat alone in the grim family room. Her hands in her lap, tears streaming from her clear blue eyes, she looked like Botticelli's Madonna. Her golden hair warmed the dingy room heavy with people's misery.

"I'm sorry, Faith."

"It's OK. We were no longer together anyhow."

"Still, it must be hard for you."

"It is. But after he killed all those people..."

Emma gasped. The suspicions hanging over Carlos weren't public knowledge. How did Faith know? What did she know?

"Which people?"

"The patients."

"What makes you think he killed patients?"

"Who else, if not him?"

Emma shrugged.

"It must be him. He was involved with all of them, one way or another. He killed them, one by one. Then he could no longer stand the remorse. Or maybe got afraid of getting caught. That's why he tried to commit suicide. That's what that accident was about."

Emma's jaw fell. She didn't think Carlos had killed the patients. There was no reason to believe that the accident was a suicide attempt. *But then, I barely know him. Faith does. They lived together for years. She knows him better than anybody.*

And she hates him.

"I don't know, Faith. It doesn't sound like the Carlos I know. I think he's a decent man."

In a flash, Faith turned dark. Eyes spitting fire, she stood up to pace.

"You're right. You don't know. I do. Did you know he was only twelve when he joined a gang? He was fourteen the first time he got arrested? He's a criminal. He's always been a criminal. That's who he is."

Fists tight, head forward, Faith paced the small room. Back and forth, back and forth. Like a caged animal.

"He puts on a good face. He pretends to be nice. He acts like he cares about you. But he'll throw you under the bus if it suits him. That's what he did to me. He threw me away. Me!"

Eyes wild, black painted nails digging into her palms, Faith choked with rage.

Filled with unease, Emma leaned back. *She has nothing good to say about him, even as he's dying. No tears, no regrets. Nothing but hate.*

She waited and waited for Faith's anger to die down. It didn't.

"Faith, would you like me to call somebody for you? A friend? A priest? How about getting you something to help you relax?"

Suddenly, Faith's fury vanished. She smiled like nothing had ever happened. She took Emma's hand.

"Oh, no. Thank you, Dr. Steele, I'll be all right. I was just surprised. You're right, Carlos is a good man. I'm heartbroken that this happened to him! He couldn't have killed all those people. Thank you for talking to me."

"Of course." Emma forced herself to hug her, then rushed out. Touching Faith made her skin crawl. She went back to work. She saw the dog bite in Room 4, the drunk in 7 and the broken ankle in 12.1. She forgot about Carlos and Faith, until the phone call.

"I thought you'd like to know how he is," Dr. Roth said.

"Of course."

"He's made it this far. We had to do a pericardial window. It was good that you didn't intubate, he had a pneumothorax too. His spleen was shattered. He made it by the skin of his teeth. For now."

"How about his head?"

"Not much on the CT. No fracture, no bleed. We'll see if

he wakes up. We'll lighten up the sedation tomorrow. If he makes it that far."

"Thanks for calling, Dr. Roth. I appreciate it."

"My pleasure. I hope I'll see you around."

Emma smiled and hung up. She ordered antibiotics for the pneumonia in Room 14 and signed out.

69

I t was still early when Emma's phone woke her up the next morning. They needed her at the hospital. She brushed her teeth, threw on a set of clean scrubs, and left.

Mike, Gus, and Sal were waiting in Mike's office.

"What's up?"

"Your patient? Room 14? Yesterday?

The pneumonia I admitted before I left.

"Yes?"

"He died."

"Really? He wasn't that sick! How come?"

"He died from a morphine overdose."

"Morphine? Who gave him morphine?"

"You did."

"I did not. He was not in pain."

Mike's eyes were hard as rocks as he looked at her. He turned the computer screen to show her the chart. Clear as daylight: 50 mg of morphine. Her order.

That's impossible.

She looked again. Yep. Her order.

"I didn't order this."

They stared at her.

"Mike, I didn't order this. This is insane! Why should I order 50 mg of morphine? I never, in my life, gave more than 10 at any one time! And this patient wasn't even in pain!"

"This is your patient. This is the order. This is your electronic signature."

"I did not order this."

Gus stared like he'd never seen her before. Mike frowned. And Sal...Sal's eyes didn't meet hers.

"That's not what the computer says," Gus said.

"What time was it?"

"3:45," Sal said.

Just before the end of my shift. I was still in the ER. Except that I didn't do it.

"Who gave it?" Emma asked. *No nurse in her right mind would give such a monstrous order.*

Sal shrugged. "It's not marked."

"Who was his nurse?" Mike asked.

"George," Emma said.

I didn't put in that order. And George would never give it.

"We'll speak to him. Can I have a moment with Dr. Steele?" Gus asked.

Mike and Sal left, closing the door behind them.

"Emma, how much do you drink?"

Emma's stomach fluttered. A wave of nausea hit her.

"Nothing, ever, when I work."

"Still, how much do you drink?"

"I don't see how that's any of your business."

"Actually, it is. I wonder how much your drinking interferes with your work. As ED director, you're practically always on call. Even in your off hours. As such, you're actually drinking on call."

Emma's anger blew through her like a dark wind. Her throat tightened.

"I know you have a lot of stress. The job is stressful. Your personal life hasn't been easy. Ken's death. Victor. Taylor. All that takes its toll." He paused, waiting for an answer.

One-two-three. One-two-three. Emma counted her breaths in an effort to slow her heart rate. She crossed her arms tightly on her chest, to prevent herself from punching him.

"However, we cannot allow your personal problems to interfere with the care and the safety of our patients. You are becoming a liability for the department. You need to put your life in order."

Emma's teeth clenched so hard she could hear them crack.

"I'll give you one week. Sort out your personal life. Consider detox. There are many upscale, discreet facilities. You could turn your life around."

Emma knew a lot about detox facilities. She had researched them for Taylor, who'd eloped from one only weeks ago. She didn't need detox. Her drinking was *her* problem. Nobody else's. She hadn't ordered that morphine. She never drank on the job. She'd never drink and drive. Somebody was sinking her. She remembered George: *"I have a feeling something bad is about to happen to you, Emma."*

He was right.

70

The house was quiet when Emma got home that evening. She walked from the kitchen to Taylor's room, then to her own bedroom, where Guinness slept on her bed when she thought nobody knew. Nobody home. She went to the wine rack.

"If you drink, you are drinking on call."
So what?

She was always on call. She'd been on call for months. Ever since the blasted day they made her director. Her drinking never interfered with her work. If anything, it helped. Thinking of her wine had sustained her through many nasty encounters with patients, consultants, and staff. Instead of blowing up, she'd smile and nod, thinking: *Stupid motherfucker. You're not worth getting in trouble for. I'll reward myself with a better wine tonight for keeping calm as I talk to you. Like now.*

It feels like a night to celebrate. What? I'm not sure. Being alive? Figuring out who the killer is? Having a quiet moment? Between the ER, Taylor, and Guinness, that's as rare as hen's teeth.

She chose a 2004 Brunello de Montalcino. A very special Italian wine. She'd fallen in love with it by mistake. She and Victor were in Rome for their honeymoon. Thanks to Margret, they stayed at an exclusive hotel near the Pantheon, so posh that the doorman intimidated them.

They made love. They slept, embraced. They woke up at midnight, hungry. Rome was asleep. They had to make do with the stale sandwiches in the room and the bottle of expensive Brunello they'd bought for Margret.

"We'll buy her another," Victor said.

They sat together on the windowsill, their thighs touching. They watched the moon pour gold over the Pantheon. They ate stale salami sandwiches and drank Brunello from each other's lips. They talked. They made love. They watched the darkness swallow Rome when the moon hid behind the buildings. Brunello had tasted like love, magic, and Rome ever since.

Emma opened the bottle. It surrendered with a wet "pop." She poured the blood of the grapes in a long-stemmed glass. She sat on the green leather sofa, put her feet up, and sniffed the wine. *Cherry, strawberry, and walnut.*

Walnut? She took a second nose. *Walnut. Enough foreplay.* She took a healthy sip. She closed her mouth around the wine, allowing it to bathe her tongue, the inside of her cheeks, her palate. She chewed on it, driving it into the farthest corners of her mouth, imbibing every taste bud. She swallowed. She focused on the lingering finish pleasuring her mouth even after the wine was gone. Like the glow of the sunset, still there after the sun is gone.

She sat alone staring at the dark TV screen, thinking. About Rome. About Victor. About how marriages fail and love dies. About Vincent.

That's when our marriage died. It died the morning when Vincent didn't wake up.

He woke her up every night, then every morning before dawn, asking to feed. Except that night. Her full, heavy breasts woke her up that morning. He'd never slept through the night. He hadn't this time either. He had been dead for hours. His eyes were open, his face purple, his tiny body stiff as a board. Emma did mouth to mouth. Victor called the ambulance and took Taylor away. Nothing helped. Vincent was dead, and their marriage died with him. For a while, they pretended it was still alive. They were still together, but they each grieved alone. Almost.

Emma turned to wine. Victor turned to Amber.

Amber's pregnancy sealed the deal. She was going to give Victor his son back.

Emma was empty.

Amber had a girl.

Emma had nothing. Nothing, but hundreds of nights waking up in a cold sweat to check that Taylor was still breathing. It took her a year to come alive again. Not fully alive—a piece of her got buried with Vincent. More alive than not.

That was long ago. Too long to remember how it used to feel being a whole person. She survived Vincent's death thanks to wine. Emma knew she was an alcoholic. She drank every day. She never drank before work. She never drank and drove. But she loved wine. Wine was always there when she needed it. He never failed to soothe her, warm her, release her inhibitions, dull her pain. Wine made her feel relaxed, smart, and funny. Wine silenced her mother's voice, that voice inside her telling her that she was never good enough, smart enough, successful enough. She never worked hard enough.

Wine allowed the real her—the carefree, funny, life-loving person inside her—to come out. Life would be untenable without it. At work, she was the straight-laced, never-give-up doctor that she was, thanks to coffee. She always did the best she could. At home, she got to be herself. She ditched the bitchy conscience her mother had beaten into her. She felt less empty, less alone, less of a failure. She couldn't let go of her wine. She'd rather let go of her job.

Wine was her lifeline. She shivered thinking about how her life would be without wine. She didn't want to know. She poured the last of the bottle thinking about Boris. Handsome, charming, futureless Boris, who had stopped drinking.

She drank to his health.

71

"Dr. Steele to Room 3."

Emma was happy to leave Room 7. He didn't want to wait for his results. He wanted a sandwich and a taxi voucher, and he wanted them now. Emma shrugged. *I'll send the caseworker. I hope she can deal with him.*

Her stomach turned as she stepped in Room 3. Nausea became dizziness. She had to lean on the sink to let it pass. She took a deep breath. *Seriously? I knew that life's always there to kick you in the ass, but I didn't know it had such impeccable timing!*

The patient in Room 3 was Boris. Boris, chalk-white, still smiling.

"Hello, Emma. I couldn't stay away."

"I guess not. What happened?"

He smiled. The dried blood around his mouth made him look like Dracula's cousin. "This happened." He pointed at his blood-covered shirt.

"When did this start?" Emma asked, her thoughts racing furiously. She shouldn't be involved with his case. It was too personal. She should ask somebody else to care for him. But the other doctors were busy. And she couldn't leave him. Not now, when he needed her. Not ever.

"Last night. I hoped it would stop. It didn't."

Emma wanted to slap him and hug him, all at the same time.

"What do we have for IV access?"

"An eighteen in the right AC," Judy said. "Working on a second."

"Thanks. I'll put in orders."

She smiled and left the room, biting her lip to keep from crying. She ordered labs, she ordered blood, she paged GI. She went back.

So pale he looked transparent, his blond hair stiff with blood, he smiled when he saw her.

"There's something about you, Emma. It's like the sun comes up when you enter the room. I'm glad I got to tell you this. Don't ever forget it. You are the light."

Emma's throat tightened. She was about to burst out crying. She wondered what the nurses thought. Then his expression changed. His eyes closed, he bent over the side of the bed. A fountain of blood came out of him. Then another.

He leaned back and smiled again.

"I wish we had more time. I wish we met years ago, when I was a man and a lover, not this grotesque caricature of myself, waiting to die. I wish I could be with you then, now, and forever. Would you have married me?"

"Why don't you wait and ask me later?" Emma laughed, her heart in shreds. "I'll have to think about it. I'm a little busy now. I have a patient to care for."

He smiled again, but the light in his eyes was fading.

"There is no later, Emma. This is it. I know it. You know it too."

His eyes closed for a moment, his blood-splattered face calm, too calm. Dead calm.

He opened his eyes and caught Emma's hand.

"I'm glad I met you anyhow. Even now. My life was brighter because of you, Emma, my light."

He let go and bent over again. He bled, and bled, and bled.

I didn't know one human can have so much blood. Five liters? It feels like five hundred.

Years later, when the GI arrived, he glanced at Boris. He frowned.

"What did you give him?"

"Everything. Blood, Protonix, TXA, octreotide. I tubed him for airway protection. I started the massive transfusion protocol."

He shook his head, his mouth a thin line.

Blood spurted out around the tube. Thick and opaque, blood covered the camera, hiding the bleeder. There was no way to find it. There was no way to stop it. They gave units after units of red cells, plasma, and platelets to replace the puddles on the floor. That kept him alive a little longer. But the only way to save him was to stop the bleeding.

They couldn't do it.

Intervention radiology would help, but there was none in-house.

Surgery would help, but the surgeon was in a complicated trauma case.

The second surgeon came. Too late.

Boris died. With him, another piece of Emma's heart. She'd fallen for this brilliant, charming, terminal Russian like she hadn't fallen in a long time.

Her heart heavy, her eyes burning, she called Vera. She didn't want to tell her.

She didn't have to. Vera knew.

She arrived minutes later. She hugged Emma, her eyes bright with tears.

"I'm sorry, Vera. I couldn't save him. I tried."

"I know. There was no saving him, Emma. His chances died when he drank away his liver, years ago. It just took him a while to catch up."

She didn't know how she went through the rest of her shift.

Back home, that night, Emma looked at her wine with fear and longing.

Am I really killing myself?

She didn't know. Even worse, she didn't care. *Who cares if I die? Nobody, really. Vincent is gone. Taylor is pretty much on her own. Victor has Amber. Boris died today.*

She shrugged. *If I kill myself, may as well do it in style.* She picked her most expensive wine: A bottle of 2012 Domaine des Comtes Lafon Meursault 1er Cru 'Les Perrieres... mineral notes that need some encouragement... citrus peel, walnut, and smoke with a long peacock's tail on the finish that reasserts its position as the most propitious premier cru'. *Propitious? I can use that. Today more than ever. Encouragement too. These wine people have a way with words!*

She sniffed it. She lifted the glass to her lips.

Guinness barked. Sitting facing her, staring in her eyes, she barked again.

She lay her head in Emma's lap.

Tears burned Emma's eyes. "You're right. You care."

She poured the wine back, recorked it, and went to bed.

72

ANGEL

I'm disappointed, Emma. I thought we were friends.

For you, I did things I never did for anybody else. I did things nobody else did for you.

I deserve gratitude, but you gave me the cold shoulder instead.

People don't give me the cold shoulder. Not for long!

That morphine was just a little warning. I hope you got the message.

I'll give you another chance. One more.

You should take it. Or you'll be sorry.

Look at Carlos. Don't you think he's sorry?

If he isn't, he should be. And it's not over. His fun is just about to begin.

Take care, Emma! Make good choices!

I'd hate to lose you!

73

That night, Emma spent hours awake in her bed. Without wine to dull her senses and help her through her misery, her heart felt like a huge hole. A void, sucking her. She was the center of pain. Inside her there was nothing but loss.

She felt foolish to be so distraught about losing somebody she had only met a few times. She barely knew Boris. He wasn't really part of her life. But he taught her hope. He told her that she was worthy and beautiful just the way she was. She felt worthy and beautiful with him. Now that he was gone, she was back to feeling useless and empty. She hadn't been able to save him. She did her best to be a good doctor, a good mother, a decent human being. She failed, more often than not.

She got up to pour herself a glass of milk. Guinness followed, so she poured her one too. They sat on the green sofa, looking at the black windows. She needed to refocus. Give her brain a task. Feeling sorry for herself wasn't getting her anywhere. May as well think about something useful.

She thought about Carlos. She remembered Faith saying

that he killed those patients, then, driven by remorse, tried to kill himself.

"That's bullshit. That girl is crazy. Batshit crazy. Is she the one who's framing Carlos? She has a motive. She's mad that he ditched her. Let's say it was her. How would she do it?"

Guinness cocked her head, listening with rapt attention.

"Getting his ID and PIN is a piece of cake. They lived together for years. She knows everything about him. She got in the system under his ID and used his PIN to sign that he gave those meds. Still, those meds weren't enough to kill his patient. So she gave him more, then signed as Carlos."

Guinness laid her head back on her paws, her ears up. She kept listening, waiting for her favorite words — walk, ball, frisbee, eat, bacon. Not coming.

"Giving fentanyl to the woman with the broken hip was a piece of cake. Same with the morphine for the patient in Room 15. She looked so peaceful and relaxed when I went to see her. I thought she was doing better. Instead, she was dying, overdosed on morphine. Taylor's patient? That was the easiest. It was Faith's patient too. She knew Carlos had just been there. She pretended to flush her IV, but she pushed the propofol instead. But how did she get the vial?"

Guinness had no idea, and didn't care. By now she was asleep.

"She stole the kit. She waited until Carlos left the room, then stepped in and grabbed it. But Carlos had signed that he discarded it. What if it wasn't Carlos? It was Faith, signed in as Carlos."

It all makes sense. She could do every one of these things. But that doesn't mean that she did. I have no proof. What if I'm wrong? What if I accuse an innocent person, a friend who saved my life, of something so horrific?

In her heart, Emma knew she was right. That had to be the truth, even if she couldn't prove it.

How can I prove it? Follow her. Where? That's silly. I don't know how to do that. Check her house? There may be something there. Drugs, or Carlos's ID. But how do I get in? And what if I get caught? I'll speak to Carlos. He's got to know something.

I could try to catch her in the act. Who would she go for next? Carlos. She hates him. He knows things about her. She already said that Carlos tried to kill himself. He's in the hospital, sick. He's an easy target.

Carlos may be next.

74

A few hours into her shift, and many more left to go, Taylor didn't feel well. She needed a break, but they were busy. She couldn't leave Faith to deal with everything by herself. She was going to push through.

Something to eat, or at least something to drink, would help, but they weren't allowed food or drinks at the desk. The administrators, bless their hearts, didn't like it. What if JCAHO, the hospital accreditation committee, came for an unannounced visit? They could get cited for irregularities. Maybe even fined. Better keep the staff hungry and thirsty.

Taylor got the urine specimen from Room 6. *Urine is always hard to get. You'd think you were asking for gold.* She sent it to the lab, then went to draw blood in Room 5. She got dizzy. She held on to the corner of the desk. She waited a moment, then headed to Room 5.

The next thing she knew, she lay on a stretcher. Worried faces looked down at her.

"Are you OK?" Faith asked.

"Yes, thanks." Taylor tried to get up.

They held her down.

"Stay right there. We need to check you out," Dr. Crump said.

"I'm OK, really. I just got up late and missed breakfast. Then I didn't drink enough."

"Does your neck hurt?"

"No."

"How about your head?"

"It's fine."

They checked her out. Everything looked good.

"You need some fluids," Dr. Crump said. "Faith, let's get an IV and give her a liter."

"No, thanks, I'm OK, I can drink." Taylor hated needles.

"Will you drink a liter?"

"I will."

She did.

An hour later, Dr. Crump stopped by to see her. Eric had dropped in. He ran back to the ICU to his patients.

"Nice young man," Dr. Crump said. "Is he..." He looked at her belly.

Taylor blushed.

"He's my fiancé."

Dr. Crump smiled.

Taylor felt that she owed him more.

"Dr. Crump, regarding our conversation the other day..."

"Yes."

"There's something you need to know." She took a deep breath, forcing herself to say it. "When I became pregnant, my boyfriend at the time and I, we were doing drugs. A lot of drugs."

"I see," Dr. Crump said, his face darkening.

"I haven't done any in months, but I don't know how this has affected the baby. He may not be normal. I thought you should know."

"I know. Still, thanks for telling me, Taylor."

"It wasn't Eric."

Faith came to get her vitals. She attached the blood pressure cuff to her arm.

"What do you mean?" he asked.

"The baby's father. It's not Eric."

"I know," he said. "It's Dr. Umber."

The IV cart crashed with a bang.

75

Carlos opened his eyes. He didn't recognize the place. He couldn't remember how he got there. He looked around. Suspended ceiling. White walls. A window, framing an aspen. That reminded him of something. Something scary.

He tried to sit up. He couldn't.

There was something in his mouth. He tried to take it out.

His right hand didn't move. He tried the left. That didn't move either.

Where am I? he screamed, but no sound came out.

Things beeped. Alarms rang. Somebody came.

A young man. Blond. In scrubs.

"Carlos? I'm Eric, your nurse. You're in the ICU."

Carlos's eyes shouted a question. Eric heard it.

"You were in a car accident. Do you remember?"

Night. Rain. Long road. Running away. Trying to escape. Changing my mind. Coming back. Then the left turn. The aspen.

He blinked yes.

"Good. You're doing much better. You hit your head. You

were in a coma for days. You also had chest injuries. You had to have a pericardial window and a chest tube. They took out your spleen because you were bleeding inside. You understand?"

Carlos blinked.

"I'll tell Dr. Roth you're awake. He'll be happy to hear. Now that you're awake, they'll look into extubating you. I'm sure you'd rather have this tube out of your throat."

You don't know how much.

"You've had a lot of visitors," Eric said, showing him a pile of "Get Well Soon" cards. "George, Brenda, Dr. Steele, Taylor, Faith. They all asked me to call them if there's any change."

Carlos frowned and shook his head no.

"You don't want me to call them?"

He shook his head again.

"None of them?"

Carlos blinked.

"Which one? George? Faith? Dr. Steele?"

Blink.

"OK. I'll call her. She was here only this morning."

She came an hour later, dressed in her faded scrubs as usual. The scrubs looked tired. She did too, her hair in a messy knot, her lipstick gone, her eyes bloodshot. She smiled when she saw him awake.

"Carlos! I'm so happy to see you! We were worried we lost you!"

Who's we?

She heard the unspoken question. "The ED folks. George, Brenda, Taylor, me, many others. How are you?"

He shrugged.

"I have something for you."

She took out a notebook and a pen. She sat them on his

chest. His hands were loosely tied to stop him from pulling out his ET tube. She untied them.

"There. You can talk now."

He laughed. He heard a gurgle inside his throat. The alarms went crazy. She laughed.

"I guess laughing is alarming, here in the ICU. I'll keep that in mind."

Carlos took the pen. He bent his knees to support the notebook. His stiff, unsteady fingers, scribbled huge drunk letters. Four words covering the whole sheet.

"I didn't do it."

"Do what?"

"Kill them."

"I know. I never thought you did."

Peace spread inside him. There was at least one person who knew he was innocent. He thought they were all against him.

"The question is: Who did? Do you know?"

Carlos closed his eyes, thinking. He opened them and shook his head.

"You don't?"

No.

"Are you sure?"

No.

"You don't really want to know."

Carlos said nothing.

"I think I do. I have a theory, but I have no proof," Emma said. "I need your help."

What?

"Say, just for the sake of the argument, that Faith had something really important to hide. Something that nobody should ever find. Where would she put it?"

Carlos frowned.

"You don't think it's her?"

Tears streamed down his cheeks leaving a shiny path. They dropped, darkening his pillow.

"You don't want it to be her?"

Carlos closed his eyes. He was tired. He didn't want to hear what she had to say. He didn't want to think what she suggested. He was heartbroken.

But she was right. He opened his eyes again, grabbed the notebook, and scribbled: "My stuff."

"Your stuff."

He nodded. If Faith wanted to hide something that nobody would find, and even if they found it, it wouldn't incriminate her, she'd put it in with his stuff. The boxes he failed to recover were still in her spare room. It was a no-brainer to put it there, whatever "it" was. If anyone found it, she'd say he left it there. Faith was a smart girl. She knew damn well how to play her cards.

She'd played him pretty well.

76

The following morning Emma went back to work after another sleepless night. She worried about Carlos. She wondered how to keep him safe.

She had asked Eric to keep an eye on him. He stared at her as if she'd lost it.

"Of course. I keep both eyes on him, every shift, all the time."

She had dropped it. *What else can I say? Watch out for his ex? She's an ER nurse. Nice girl. She may try to kill him.*

Back from seeing Room 4, Emma found Faith waiting. She had brought coffee and stopped for a chat. She smiled, friendly as always, but Emma had trouble looking her in the eye.

"How about a spa day tomorrow? I have some coupons."

"Sorry, Faith, I can't do tomorrow."

"The day after tomorrow?"

"No, sorry, I can't. I'm working," she said. She remembered that the schedule was posted in the office.

Faith will see I'm not on it. She'll think I lied. She won't know that I have administrative work. Oh well. It was time to cool it down anyhow.

Faith hugged her and left. Emma shuddered, threw away the coffee she had brought and went back to work. She rechecked her orders once more. She'd gotten paranoid since that monstrous morphine order. She hadn't done it—but maybe a typo? She mis-clicked? She'd tried to order 50 mg of Benadryl or metoprolol and she somehow clicked the wrong box?

Deep inside she knew she hadn't, but her old self-doubt was back. There was no explanation for it. It had to be her fault.

She'd been thinking about Carlos. She replayed their "conversation" in her head over and over. *He still cares about Faith. He's not sure she's the killer.*

Emma wasn't sure either, but she was getting close. She had no better explanation. In the meantime, she watched her back.

She rechecked her orders again: steroids, nebs, Zithromax. Nothing there to kill anyone. She signed them. She logged off and went to see the shoulder pain in Room 9.

He was riding a motorbike when he slipped and ran into a ditch. He fell off and dislocated his shoulder. The deformity was obvious. The left shoulder was muscular and rounded, the right sharply squared. His other hand immobilized his hurt arm. His eyes widened as Emma got close.

He doesn't want me anywhere near that shoulder.

She sat by his side, keeping her hands to herself. He got back to breathing.

"Does anything else hurt? Your neck? Your back?"
"No."

"Did you hit your head? Did you pass out?"
"No."

"Can you move your fingers?"

Still watchful, he did. He looked good other than the shoulder. Emma ordered an X-ray. He looked relieved that she kept her word and didn't touch him. *Good. I need him to work with me to put that shoulder back. If not, I'll have to sedate him. That takes time and resources. Plus, with all this shit going on, I'm afraid to do it.*

"I'll get you something for pain. It will help with the X-ray too." She ordered Toradol, then reluctantly added 50 micrograms of fentanyl. *They'll take the edge off but they can't hurt him.* She checked the order, then rechecked it. She signed it.

She rounded on her patients once more. She checked on them often, since she was always afraid to find them dead. *They're all breathing.* The chest pain with the wonky EKG in Room 5 looked OK. Room 4 was breathing better after nebs.

"Dr. Steele to Room 9."

Her heart quickened. She dashed to Room 9.

The kid was blue. George was bagging, Amy was doing CPR, Judy brought in the code cart.

"What happened?"

The X-ray tech, , a nice brown woman with gray hair, could hardly speak. "I came to take him to X-ray. He didn't look right. He wasn't breathing. I called for help."

"Did he have a pulse?"

She shrugged.

"No pulse," George said, "at least none that I could feel."

Emma wanted to cry. She wanted to scream. She wanted to throw a massive temper tantrum. She didn't.

"Epi. And Narcan," she said.

"How much?"

"Two."

They gave it. Nothing happened.

"Two more."

Nothing.

After the third dose, the pulse came back. His face turned pink. He started breathing.

Emma grabbed his right arm, bent his elbow for leverage and pulled the arm away. She rotated it outwards, extending it above his head. The shoulder fell back into its socket with a thunk. He opened his eyes.

"That was cool," George said.

"Yes!" Amy nodded.

"Yep, but what the hell happened?" Judy asked.

Emma shrugged. She didn't know what happened. The one thing she knew was that she was toast. Another patient who coded for no reason. Her patient. There was no explaining this away. She was already on notice. This was it.

She signed in to check his chart. Her orders stared her in the face: X-ray, Toradol, fentanyl. Just like she wrote them. Except the fentanyl. She had ordered 50 micrograms of fentanyl. She had rechecked it twice. Now, it was 500 micrograms. Ten times the dose she had ordered. Her signature.

How the hell did that happen? Have I really lost it? Am I going crazy?

That evening she took her stuff with her. She didn't think she'd be back for tomorrow's shift.

She was right. The VPM called her that evening.

"What happened?"

She told him.

"Your order?"

"Yes."

"Sorry, Emma. There's nothing I can do. Time for you to take a breather."

She was put on leave while they investigated. They'd let her know.

"I think I've lost it," Emma said. "I really checked that order. I thought I did."

Guinness understood. She was ready to help. She went to the kitchen and came back with the leash.

"How's that supposed to help?" Emma asked.

Guinness went to the door.

"I know what it's for. I'm asking you how do you think it's helpful?"

Guinness barked.

"A little exercise will do you good. Come on! I need to check my email. And I need to pee."

"Oh well. We may as well. I need the exercise, and it helps me think. And I think it's high time I did some thinking." Emma laughed.

Guinness cocked her head.

"You've lost it."

77

In the ICU, Carlos opened his eyes and looked at the window. He could barely make up the aspen, but the fading sky told him that sunrise was just minutes away. It was his last day there. They were going to extubate him today, and move him to a regular floor.

He remembered everything, and a tear ticked his left cheek. He tried to wipe it away, but his hands were still tied. The ties were long enough to let him write on the notebook in his lap, without letting him reach his tube.

The door opened.

Faith smiled. She bent over and kissed his forehead, then pulled a chair and sat.

"How are you doing, honey? I missed you."

Her finger traced the line of his jaw, the curve of his ear, the hollow in his throat.

I must be dreaming,

He turned his head. Door to the left. Window to the right. Machines beeping everywhere. The tube in his throat.

I'm not dreaming. God can't be so cruel as to make me dream my ICU imprisonment. And Faith. This is real.

He wished he could ask. He remembered his notebook.

"Why?" he scribbled.

"I missed you. I came to say good-bye. Remember our good old days? We were in love, you and I. You were the only one in the world for me. I was the only one in the world for you. Nobody else mattered." Her smile melted. Her eyes became ice shards.

"You had to spoil it all by obsessing about Dick."

Me? I spoiled it? By obsessing about Dick?

"Yes. Everything would have been fine if you didn't act out."

Carlos stared.

"Then, when father got sick, you didn't support me. You were so wrapped up in your jealousy that you didn't even hear me ask for help. Remember when I told you I couldn't bear it anymore?"

Her eyes left his face. She stared at her ring, twisting it around her finger.

My ring. She's still wearing it.

"It was horrendous. All that screaming. Day and night. Screaming. No sleep, no food, no peace, nothing but screaming. All the time. It drove me crazy. It inhabited my dreams. It woke me up from sleep. It got my food stuck in my throat. I couldn't bear it anymore."

She pushed her silky golden hair behind her ears and leaned back in her chair. She crossed her legs, showing off the sharp line of her ironed green scrubs. He'd never seen anyone ironing scrubs before Faith.

"I had to do something!"

She stared at him, her eyes open so wide the white showed all around the blue. Carlos shivered.

"His doctor prescribed morphine. He refused it. He wanted to show God he was worthy. I tasted it. It was sweet. I thought about baking him a cake. 'He won't eat enough of it,' I thought. Ice cream? I don't know how to make ice cream. I made Jell-O. Morphine Jell-O. Ever had morphine Jell-O?" She laughed.

"Me neither. I flavored it with almond extract. It smelled like cyanide, but it wasn't. It was morphine. He loved it. I gave him more. He fell asleep. I poured the rest of the morphine down his throat. He choked, but he was too zonked to care."

She smiled.

"He stopped screaming."

Carlos shivered.

"I tried to tell you, but you wouldn't listen. You kept on about Dick. About me dragging you here. Like it mattered! All that mattered was that I stopped the screaming. I helped the nasty old bastard! What a shit he was! With his God, his crappy death, and his nasty attitude toward life. The son of a bitch ruined my life, my mother's life, and his own life, the stupid, bigoted piece of shit. Did you listen? No. You left me."

She sobbed.

"I tried to be understanding. You were upset. Your manliness was threatened. I gave you time."

Carlos broke into a cold sweat.

"Something had changed in me when I came back. All those old people suffering. It hurt. It made me relive the nightmare with Father. I couldn't stand it. Then it dawned on me. I could help. I had some fentanyl left over from Dick. I gave it to her. I freed her from her pain. She was grateful to die. She called me an angel. I had made a difference."

Her eyes returned to him.

"I was happy. I was so happy I gave you a second chance.

I took you back in my life. Back in my bed. And you? You ran away. That was stupid."

Her eyes darkened with anger.

"You said I'm disgusting. I disgust you, you, dirty little spic! I had to punish you. I killed your patient. The back pain. Yes, it was me."

"They came after you. I let you take the fall. It would be fun to see you in jail, I thought. What if they put you in with Dick? You two have a lot in common. But then you ran away again, you bastard. You ran away again!"

Faith smiled.

"You didn't make it far. It's good to see you again, honey."

She caressed his cheek and straightened his hair. "You've always had nice hair. You need a shower though. Don't worry, they'll wash you afterwards."

She leaned over to kiss his forehead. Her perfume, chocolate, jasmine, and honey, got through to him, in spite of the tube in his throat.

Sweet and intoxicating.

"It was nice talking to you, but I have to go. I just wanted to say good-bye."

He stared at her, his eyes wide. She understood.

"Oh, I don't know. I'll figure it out. Wherever the wind takes me. But I have to take my baby first."

She opened her red bag.

I gave it to her for Christmas. It was a month's salary, but it was worth it. She loved it.

She took out a syringe. Carlos' heart skipped a beat.

"It won't hurt. It's going to be all right. You won't feel anything, I think."

"Why?"

He couldn't scream. He couldn't run. He couldn't move.

She knew.

She laughed.

"Are you kidding? You didn't think I was going to let you live after telling you? I wouldn't anyhow. But look at the bright side: You got to understand what happened. I bet you racked your brains trying to figure it out. Now you know. You can die happy."

She attached the syringe to his IV. She pulled the plunger to check the line. It flashed red. It worked. She looked him in the eye. She smiled and pushed the plunger in the whole way. She detached the syringe and dropped it in her bag.

Sick with fear, Carlos stared.

"What is it? Surprise."

She waved, then left closing the door.

Carlos waited. Nobody came.

The terror filled him like darkness. He was dying. He knew he was dying. He didn't even get to clear his name. She was going to get away with it, like she did with all the other murders.

I need to tell them I didn't do it. She did it. The notebook.

His heart fluttered. His eyes got blurry, as if he was under water. He blinked to clear them. It didn't work. The world became a blur.

He scribbled blindly on the notepad.

His heart fluttered again, like a bird locked in his chest, trying to fly out.

His brain fogged. He forgot what he was writing.

He forgot he was writing.

He forgot he was...

78

Down in the ER, Taylor checked her watch. The end of her shift was getting close. She straightened her back. It hurt. So did her feet, especially at the end of a twelve-hour shift. But, all in all, she was doing better. She hardly ever got sick any more. Just the opposite. She lived thinking about food. She started drooling, imagining a succulent burger. Biting into it with her mouth fully open. Juices running down her chin. She swallowed her saliva. Two more hours. Then she was going to Burger King. She'd get a Double Whopper. With cheese. No. Two. She started drooling again. She took a sip of water, wishing it was a smoothie. She got back to work.

Today she worked with Faith. Faith was nice. Since she'd heard that Umber was her baby's father, she'd been even nicer.

The day Taylor passed out, Faith sat with her.

"It must be hard for you. So young, pregnant and alone."

"I'm not alone."

"But he's...he's not here."

"I have Eric."

"Yes, but it's not the same thing. He's not your baby's father."

"No, but he's a good man and a good friend."

"You're so brave! Do you miss him?"

"Umber?"

"Yes," Faith said.

Taylor didn't miss him. *I hope he rots in hell. I hope his jail mates cut off his dick and make him eat it.* He had lied to her. He had betrayed her. He was the scum of the earth. A newt classified higher than Dr. Dick Umber in Taylor's book.

"No."

"Not even a little bit?"

"No."

Faith smiled and nodded. She didn't believe her, but she was exceptionally kind to Taylor, and Taylor was grateful.

She took another sip of water and went to triage to get the new patient, a large girl with purple hair and a nose-ring. She got grounded after stealing her mother's car, then threatened to kill herself when they took away her phone. Her friend called 911, so Police brought her in for an emergency mental health evaluation.

A few months ago, this could have been me. I'm no longer who I was in February, thank God. Or thank the ED. I look at this girl and I think there, but for the grace of God...

"She needs to change," Faith said.

To stop them from hurting themselves or the staff, mental health patients got changed into blue paper scrubs. Their belongings got inspected down to the last used condom, then locked away.

"I'll get the blues," Taylor said.

The clean utility room was in the back end of the department. She punched in the code, opening the heavy metal door to the cave-like, dim room. Heavy metal shelves sagged under the heavy bundles of blankets, pillows, and scrubs.

She found a large bundle of XXL blues on the bottom shelf. As she bent over to free a top, she heard the door behind her. She managed to get a top, then she struggled to break free a bottom. It wouldn't come. She pulled harder.

She felt a sting in her hip. A hand grabbed her neck and pushed her down.

She fell on top of the scrubs, her arms protecting her belly.

Hands pushed her to the ground. The weight on her back forced her into the floor. She tried to resist. She couldn't.

She rolled.

Faith, her face distorted by hate. Unblinking blue eyes, staring into hers. Feral teeth, gleaming white under rolled lips. Faith, rabid, ready to bite off her throat.

"You, miserable little bitch. You took my man. You took him and threw him away. You bitch." Her voice, low and cracked, held nothing human.

Taylor gasped. Her heart raced. Her brain too. *She lost her mind. What's she talking about? I've never been near Carlos.*

"No, Faith, I've never had anything to do with Carlos, I swear! He just helped me get those labs..."

Faith's rictus reminded her of tetanus. She'd seen pictures. *What did they call it? Risus sardonicus. It wasn't funny.*

Her arms got heavy. Her whole body did.

"You took my man, you lying slut. You took him, but you aren't going to take my baby."

Her baby?

Taylor shuddered. Her whole body went into a spasm. Then again. And again.

She couldn't move.

Faith let her go.

Taylor tried to get up, but she couldn't. Her body was too heavy.

Faith's hand reached for her pocket. She took out a scalpel.

"I'll take my baby now."

She's crazy. Totally crazy.

The scalpel descended toward Taylor's belly.

She's going to cut me to take him out! This is insane. She wanted to tell her that it was too early. The baby couldn't live out of the womb. Not yet.

It's too early. He needs at least another couple of months inside!

She couldn't speak. Her tongue was lead. Her face was heavy. Her arms weighed tons.

She couldn't move. She lay there, watching.

Faith undid the tie of Taylor's scrubs. She pulled up the top. Set free, the pink belly glowed, lighting the dark room. *Grotesque.* She took a bottle of iodine from her pocket. She opened it and splashed it over Taylor's belly, painting the skin brown.

The chemical fumes burned Taylor's eyes, but she couldn't blink. She watched the scalpel come closer. And closer.

Faith smiled. She pushed the scalpel blade open with her thumb.

Taylor's brain sank in darkness. The black engulfed her. Everything was dark, but the blade. The blade caught the meager light, reflecting it. It glistened closer and closer to her skin.

To her womb.

To her baby.

79

That morning, Emma had to force herself to return to the hospital. She hated being there. Now, that she was on leave, there was no place she'd be happier to avoid. Well, maybe the ER. But she had to see Carlos again. She needed his help. Nobody but him could help her expose Faith.

She opened the door to the ICU. The place was in chaos. Carlos's room was a cacophony of alarms, screams, and people rushing. Emma couldn't believe it. *It can't be Carlos. He was doing so well last time I saw him. We worked so hard to keep him alive.*

It was him. Dead.

A sweaty nurse moved aside from doing CPR to make room for another.

"What happened?" Emma asked.

"He coded."

Thanks, Nurse Obvious. What the hell happened?

She waited, hoping they'd bring him back.

They didn't. The intensivist called the code.

"What happened?"

He shrugged. "No idea."

Emma sighed.

There's no talking to Carlos. He can't help me anymore. Unless...

She went back to the room. They were cleaning the room, preparing it for the family.

There's no family. But Faith.

She sat in the chair by the bedside, looking at him. Dead, he looked serene. Emma remembered him alive. His passion. His troubled life. His struggles. His sorrow. His work as a nurse. The patients they saved together.

He had told her that he didn't kill their patients. As if she didn't know. *The notebook...*

"Was there a notebook?" Emma asked his nurse. "I lent it to him. I need it back."

The nurse checked the bag with his belongings: keys, belt, phone, the notebook. He handed the notebook to Emma. She grabbed it and left. She wanted the keys too, but couldn't think of a good excuse to ask for them.

I'll think of something and I'll come back

Shoulders slumped, heart heavy, she dragged herself to the cafeteria. She sat at the remote corner table, sipping on cold burned coffee. She turned the pages. Not many.

His unsteady writing on the first page: "I didn't do it."

Page two: "Kill those people."

She felt sick. *It must be the coffee.* She pushed it aside.

Communications with the nurses: "Too cold." "Turn me." "Chest hurts."

The last page said "Why?"

Emma wondered what that was about. Nurses telling him they were going to keep the tube another day? The doctor was going to be late?

Lower down, on the same page, two thin, shaky, hard-to-see letters.

"Fa..."

That could be anything. He was Catholic. He may have asked for Father O'Meara. Maybe he asked them to call his father. No, he said he never knew his father.

Fa for Faith?

Faith what?

"Faith killed me".

I'm getting ahead of myself here. But it makes sense.

I wish he'd completed that sentence.

80

Deep in thought, Emma walked slowly to her car. She didn't want to meet anyone, so she had parked far away, in the night lot parking. She didn't want people staring at her, wondering what she did to earn her disgrace. She didn't want them asking questions.

She opened the door but couldn't get in.

Something was pulling her back.

I have to go to the ER.

She slammed the door and headed back, mad at herself.

I have no business going there. I'm on leave. Everybody knows it.

Her cheeks burned with humiliation. She wanted to go home and get drunk. Very drunk. This was not about wine appreciation. This was about numbness and pain relief and forgetting that she was incompetent and useless, like Mother said.

I knew Carlos was in danger. I wanted to protect him. What a good job I did!

Deep inside her head, Mother laughed. *"It's your fault that he died. You fucked up again."*

She wanted to go home and drink. She wanted to forget how she'd fucked up her life. *That's the one good thing about Alzheimer's. You forget a lot of crap. I wish I could forget Mother.*

She didn't want to go to the ER but she had to. She didn't know why, but her gut told her to. And her gut never lied.

She punched in the code. The door opened. She wandered in, not knowing where to go. She didn't know what she was there for. People saw her and smiled. She bristled. *They're laughing at me, damn it.*

She went to the desk. Kayla was watching the cameras. a frown on her face. They covered the hallways, the med room and the mental health rooms. Kayla saw Emma and her face lit up.

"Go to the clean utility room."

Emma didn't ask why. She sprinted there and punched the code. The door opened to the gloom inside. Taylor, laying on the floor, staring at the ceiling. Faith, bent over her, holding a scalpel.

That's not how you hold a scalpel. That's how you hold a kitchen knife.

The scalpel descended toward Taylor's chest.

Not the chest. The belly.

Emma leaped forward. Faith turned.

Emma's right foot front-kicked toward the scalpel. She missed.

She got Faith's ribs instead. Faith slumped, but she didn't fall.

Emma's foot hurt. *This is different. Workouts never hurt. But of course, you hit nothing but air. Here, you need to connect.*

Eyes glued to the scalpel, she threw a right hook to Faith's cheek. She connected. A loud crack. Searing pain. *A boxer's fracture? That's going to screw up my work. Fortunately I wasn't working anyhow.*

She prepared for a left hook. She glanced at Taylor.

Why isn't she moving?

She lost sight of the scalpel. Faith slashed her arm. The deep, burning pain scorched her arm to the tip of her fingers, then back. Blood gushed.

My left has never been much good anyhow. I wish I had a weapon. A scalpel, or at least my stethoscope.

She remembered the leash. Guinness had brought it as she left. She thought they were going for a walk. Emma sent her back, rolled the heavy leash and put it in her pocket.

She pulled it out in one smooth move. The heavy metal clip flew like a bird. The air hissed. Faith's face cracked. She dropped the scalpel.

Her hand covering her face, she pivoted. Her right foot side-kicked Emma's knee from under her. The knee gave. Emma fell to the ground.

Faith bent over, picked up the scalpel, and went back to Taylor.

Emma rolled toward them. Faith ignored her. Bent over Taylor, eyes glued to her belly, she brought the scalpel to the skin. Her hand shook. She steadied it with the other.

The scalpel touched Taylor's navel.

Emma grabbed the metal linen shelf above them, and pulled on it with all her strength.

The shelf leaned, shedding heavy bundles of blankets. One fell on Faith's shoulder. She dropped the scalpel. She picked it up again.

Emma pulled harder. The shelf groaned, teetered, then crashed over Faith's back. Faith screamed.

The door opened. George, his face darker than the night. Faith saw him.

She glanced at Taylor, lying on the ground. She dropped her scalpel and ran out past him.

George's eyes followed her. He looked at Emma, kneeling, covered in blood. Three feet away, Taylor, blue and motionless, lying on the floor.

He let Faith go.

81

Emma crawled toward Taylor.

"Taylor," she heaved.

"She isn't breathing," George said.

"Pulse?"

"Yes."

Emma bent over Taylor and started mouth to mouth. George called the code.

I never kissed her on the mouth. Not even when she was a child.

She kneeled by Taylor's head and extended her neck to straighten her airway. *The only one I kissed that way was Vincent. But he was stiff.*

Taylor's body was flaccid, her blue face relaxed. Her open green eyes stared into nowhere. *Succinylcholine. Or vecuronium. Or roc. The bitch paralyzed her, and let her die.* Emma breathed another breath into Taylor's chest. She didn't have time to be angry. Not yet.

She needs oxygen. She's pregnant. They desaturate like crazy. Then the heart stops.

Another breath. *The baby. If she's not breathing, he's got no oxygen either.*

I won't think about this. Not now. Breath in, breath out, breath in...

"I got her, Emma," George said.

He had the mask with the blue bag attached.

Emma grabbed the mask and placed it on Taylor's face.

George started bagging.

The stretcher came. The people too.

A dozen hands lifted Taylor on the stretcher. George kept on bagging. Brenda pushed the stretcher to Room 3.

Emma tried to stand up. She couldn't. Her left knee gave.

Somebody pulled her up.

Ann.

"We got her, Emma."

Emma limped behind the stretcher to Room 3. She leaned against the sink, staying out of the way, watching.

"She has no muscle tone. She must have given her a paralytic," Emma said.

Ann nodded. "Let's intubate."

George lifted the mask. Ann grabbed the laryngoscope.

The monitor stopped beeping.

The heart had stopped.

Ann froze.

"Start CPR." Ann, her face heavy as lead, stared at the swollen belly.

She's thinking about a perimortem C-section. You have four minutes to cut a baby out of a dying mother. If she does it, they may die. If she doesn't, they may die.

Ann's eyes found Emma's, burning the question into her.

"Don't. It's too early. The baby isn't viable yet. Ventilate her. That's what she needs."

Ann nodded. She put the laryngoscope aside. They ventilated.

One hundred percent oxygen.

Epi.

Fifteen seconds or an eternity later, the beeping restarted.

She's back.

The baby? Who knows?

At least she's alive.

82

A lifetime later, Emma made it home. She struggled to open the door. Her left arm hurt. Her right hand too.

Everything hurts. But it's good to be home. It's good to be alive.

Her right hand was broken. A boxer's fracture. The 5th metacarpal, the tiny bone connecting her wrist to her pinky, was gone. Her cast went from her fingers to below her elbow. The 5-inch gash on her left arm needed 12 staples. Kurt wanted to put in stitches, but she didn't have the patience. She'd been away from home for too long, while Guinness was locked in the house.

And she needed wine.

Taylor was doing well. Physically. The paralytic wore off. She was breathing on her own. They extubated her. Her psyche? That was a different matter.

This day will haunt her forever. Paralyzed, watching an unhinged killer cutting your baby out of you? That's the stuff of horror movies.

Emma shivered. She hated horror movies. Life was horror enough.

Victor came to check on Taylor. Eric sat with her. The OB came to check on the baby. He looked all right. They kept her overnight to monitor them. Eric stayed with her.

Emma had a rough time making it to her car, with a cast on one arm, staples in the other, and a mangled knee. Victor offered to help, but she declined. She didn't need another complication. The drive home was a nightmare, but she made it. She closed the garage door and went inside. Guinness was waiting.

She'll jump out of her skin. She's been locked in for hours.

She didn't. She was polite and cautious. She sniffed every inch of her as if she read a small print newspaper.

What's she making of all these smells? Of the way I look? A cast on my right hand, a bandage on my left arm. I'm covered in blood. Mostly my own. Who am I kidding? It's all my own. I'm lucky if I gave her a bruise.

Emma let her out. She gave her water. She fed her dinner.

Guinness didn't want it. She lay by the door, pretending to be asleep, but her ears were up and the hair on her neck wasn't sleeping.

She's waiting for something? Taylor! That's what she's waiting for.

"She's not coming home tonight. She'll stay at the hospital, with Eric."

Guinness thumped her tail once. "OK." She went back to waiting.

"You understand, Guinness? She's not coming tonight."

She doesn't. She's just a dog, for God's sake. German, to boot. How would she understand? She's worried about Taylor. Nothing I can do. Unless...

Emma went to Taylor's room and got her sleep T-shirt. XXL, black, a red jaguar on the chest. She offered it to Guinness.

Guinness glanced at it, then went back to the door. Her long black nose on her paws, she was waiting.

"Sorry, Guinness. I can't walk you tonight. I ran out of hands. Tomorrow maybe, after Motrin."

Emma checked the wine rack. She hadn't had a glass since Boris died. That felt like a lifetime ago.

She needed wine tonight.

She needed it to clean her inside. To escape the horror, dirt, and suffering she'd been through today. In a life of daily horrors, this day took the cake.

Carlos died. He was a good man. He deserved better. He died because of this psychotic bitch.

Taylor's heart stopped in front of Emma's eyes. As for her baby? Nobody knew.

I should have destroyed Faith long ago. I knew it was her. She was behind those patient deaths. I knew it for a while. She sabotaged my career, killed half a dozen people, and almost killed Taylor, while I sat and watched. And I did nothing.Why? Because I wasn't sure.

Emma learned early that she was incompetent and useless. So, in spite of common sense, logic, and evidence, she doubted her own judgment. She couldn't have been smarter than all the others. Mike, the VPM, even Carlos— all said she was wrong.

I thought they knew better.

Instead of doing something, she'd looked for more proof. Now she had it.

It was too late. Carlos was dead, Taylor had been close. Faith had escaped. And Emma was damaged. Seriously damaged.

Wine would help her through this. Just one bottle. She needed it today.

She examined bottle after bottle, prolonging the foreplay. She found what she was looking for.

Carménère. Not subtle, like a punch in the gut isn't subtle. Dark, dry, and intense with edges you'll never find in an Australian Shiraz or a Californian pinot noir. *Pinot Noir! What an inaptly named, watered-down excuse for a red wine.*

She took a sip. She rinsed her mouth with it, exorcising the evil she'd breathed in through the day. She swallowed. She took another. The warmth entered her. It spread through her body, loving her. The wine took away the pain. It blunted the remorse. It blurred the worry.

Before too long, the bottle was empty, and the pain was gone.

I'll deal with everything tomorrow.

She called Guinness. The dog didn't come. She glanced at Emma, then thumped her tail against the floor. She went back to watching the door.

A little miffed, Emma shrugged and closed the door. *You want to sleep in the kitchen, there you go. Have at it.*

She went to her bedroom. She lay down.

Her back was grateful.

She fell asleep.

S he woke up bathed in cold sweat. She sat up, her heart racing, and stared into the darkness. *It's nothing. A nightmare. No wonder, with the day I had. Plus the wine.*

The house was dark and quiet. But there was something. She shivered.

Something evil.

A noise, almost too soft to hear. In Taylor's bedroom.

Mice?

She stood up. With soundless soft steps, she tiptoed to Taylor's room. The door was cracked open.

She wished she had a weapon. Anything. She had nothing. Her stethoscope was in her bag, on Victor's chair. Same with her scalpel. And her pepper spray.

That's silly. It's probably nothing. I'm just paranoid.

She stepped softly inside the darkness to Taylor's room.

The curtains fluttered in the night breeze.

Taylor left the windows open. That's it. The breeze moved the curtains and the windows. There I am, all bent out of shape for nothing.

She went to close the window.

An arm closed around her throat, choking her.

She bent forward to escape.

The arm's owner bent with her, laughing softly in her ear. That laughter froze her heart.

She wanted to scream. She couldn't. She could barely breathe. She thumped her bare foot to make noise. It hurt. The carpet hushed the sound.

"Where is she?" a soft voice asked in her right ear.

Emma couldn't answer if she wanted to. Not enough air through her vocal cords to speak. She didn't know what this was all about.

That's bullshit. Of course I know. It's Faith. She's come for Taylor's baby.

Police had come to the ED. They took statements from everybody. Kayla, who watched the cameras and saw Taylor heading to the utility room, then Faith following her. Emma, who'd fought her. George, who was there when she ran away.

Faith had attacked Taylor, but she was gone. They couldn't find her.

Emma had.

I wish I hadn't.

With all her strength, she pushed the arm away. She took a gulp of air. She screamed.

Guinness heard. She barked, clawing at the kitchen door.

I locked her in.

Someone may hear. Maybe.

The arm tightened again and cut her breath. It choked her scream. It made her dizzy.

Something sharp pierced Emma's throat below her right ear.

A knife. If it was a scalpel, it would be through the carotid by now. Even so, if I move, that knife will go through. She stilled.

"Where is she, I asked?"

No point in lying. She'll figure it out by herself.

"At the hospital."

"Why?"

"They're making sure your baby is OK."

A sigh warmed Emma's ear. The arm around her throat softened.

"When's she coming out?"

"Tomorrow, if the baby's OK."

"My baby."

"Tomorrow, if your baby is OK."

"I'll call him Dick."

Good name. It fits right in.

"What if it's a girl?"

The knife went in a little deeper.

"It's not a girl. My baby is a boy. You get it?"

Emma did.

"You're not a bad woman, Emma. You're even a good doctor. I learned a lot from you. Remember how you told us: Don't give insulin without glucose if they're euglycemic, or you'll kill them? Don't give opiates and benzos at the same time? Never give hypertonic saline unless they're actively seizing or in a coma?"

Emma nodded.

The arm around her neck softened.

"That's how I learned. They don't teach you how to kill people in nursing school. You learn that from the doctors. I learned from you."

How ironic.

Guinness's whining faded. *She went back to bed. I shouldn't have closed that kitchen door.*

"You were kind to me, when I was in trouble. I appreciate that. I'll be kind to you."

Kind to me?

Faith's weight drained Emma's strength. She could barely stand under their combined weight.

"I'll even let you say good-bye. Sit in that rocking chair."

Faith led her to Taylor's orange rocking chair and pushed her.

Emma fell in. She took a deep breath.

Good news: I can breathe. I can even scream. Bad news: Nobody will hear me. Escaping that chair is a challenge on a good day. Today isn't one of those.

She started circular breathing to slow down her heart. *One in—one hold—one out. Repeat.*

To escape the rocker, she had to push herself up on both hands. She didn't have two working hands. Not even one. Faith would cut her before she got up.

That's not going to happen.

Faith grabbed Taylor's leather-bound journal from the nightstand and threw it in Emma's lap. She stepped back.

She's out of reach. She has a knife.

Emma looked at the open window.

Too far.

Faith leaned against the opposite wall.

Too far.

Emma picked up Taylor's purple pen and started writing. A few seconds later she stopped and looked up.

"Did you kill Carlos?"

"Of course."

"Why?"

"He was suffering. He was a liability. I'm here to help people. I didn't want him to suffer. I didn't want him to tell anyone about me, either."

"What was there to tell?"

"Oh, you're so smart, Emma, aren't you? Trying to keep me talking. Hoping to find a way out. Not today. You have five minutes to finish. Five. That's five more than I gave Carlos. He didn't deserve them. He betrayed me. Time and time again. You were good to me. That's why I'm nice to you."

I hate to think how this would go if I wasn't.

"If I was nice to you, why kill me, Faith?"

"I'm not Faith. I'm the Angel. The Angel of Death. I'm here to help you."

"How does that help me, Angel?"

"It ends your suffering. You're old. You're fat. Your husband left you. Your daughter hates you. You're all alone. Who wants to live like that? What do you have to live for? Work? They hate you there too. I'm only trying to help you out."

This is déjà vu, all over again. Just like Mother. The worst is that it's true. She forgot that I'm an alcoholic. That would round it up nicely.

"That's generous of you, Angel. Don't you think you should ask me what I want, though?"

"No. People don't know what's good for them. They're too stupid."

Emma nodded. She'd often thought the same. She didn't take over though, like Faith was. Angel, that is.

"You have one minute left," Angel said, shifting her weight from one foot to the other. Leaning against the opposite wall, she was too far for Emma to reach.

"Then what?" Emma asked.

"I'm going to help you pass. I'll open the rainbow bridge for you. You'll be with those you love."

I'm not so sure. All those I love, except for Vincent, are still alive.

"It's time."

Faith stepped forward. Her knife, a sleek eight-inch blade, thin enough to fillet fish, was ready.

"Nice knife."

"Yes, isn't it? I love it. It's sharp, light, and smooth."

"I'd love it for cooking. Do you cook?"

"Not really, except for toast and eggs. Ready?"

"I don't know. How should I get ready?"

Angel got angry. "You've had your time. I was generous. It's over."

"Then what?" asked Emma.

Angel came closer, bending over to pick up the journal, her knife ready.

Emma rocked back and lifted her legs. She kicked as hard as she could, just under Angel's knees. Angel fell forward over Emma, knife first. Emma lifted her right arm to protect her throat. The knife came forward, all of Angel's weight behind it, piercing Emma's arm. Emma twisted. Loud as a gunshot, the knife broke, stuck in Emma's cast.

Emma rolled left with the rocker. She fell on the floor. She rolled again.

Angel rolled toward her, lifting the broken knife.

Emma tried to sit up.

Her left arm gave. She fell back.

Angel fell over her.

"I told you to be good. I was nice to you. You had to be the smart one. Again. It could have been easy for us both. One stab and done. Now it's going to hurt. It's your fault." She lifted her right arm with the broken knife and lowered it onto Emma's chest.

Blood spurted. The pain blinded her. The knife stopped in the ribs.

Emma tried to push her away. She couldn't.

She twisted and rolled over to her left, catching Angel under her.

She placed her cast over Angel's throat and pressed. Hard. With all her weight.

Angel's beautiful face turned purple.

The broken knife hit Emma's back. Searing pain took her breath away.

She kept the pressure on Angel's throat. Angel groaned.

The knife twisted between Emma's ribs, the broken tip aiming for her lungs.

She knew exactly when it got there. The pain exploded inside her chest like fireworks, blinding her. Her breath failed. Her strength vanished. Like a butterfly somebody stepped on, she shrunk, coiling into herself.

She was done. She wished she'd been better. A better person, a better doctor, a better mother. Too late. She felt sorry for all the things she failed to do. *Broken glass. Far away.*

Angel rolled over her, smiling.

"You had to make it hard, didn't you! You always make it hard for yourself. What's the good in that?" She lifted the broken knife once more. She lowered it into Emma's chest.

The ribs stopped it from reaching the heart.

She threw it down. She grabbed Emma's throat. Her thumbs pressed on the carotids.

Emma's brain darkened.

This is it. I'm gone.

The pain faded into darkness just as the window crashed open.

The pressure on her throat released. She inhaled. Her brain cleared.

Angel screamed.

Emma opened her eyes.

Guinness, dragging Angel off her by her throat.

Limp as a rag doll, Angel made no sound.

Neither did Guinness.

"Let her go! Let her go!" Emma managed, her voice so strangled she couldn't understand herself.

Guinness did.

She dropped Angel at Emma's feet like she dropped the frisbee.

Guinness looked into Emma's eyes. She licked her face.

"I told you something was wrong. You shouldn't have closed the kitchen door."

Emma's tears ran down her cheeks.

Guinness took care of them.

84

The ambulance got there first. The EMTs took in the scene. The first one went to Angel, lying motionless on the floor. The tall one grabbed his radio to ask for reinforcements.

He kneeled in front of Emma. He frowned.

"Dr. Steele?"

"Hi, Joe," she said, her voice like a coffee grinder.

His partner, Roy, was checking Angel. He heard and turned around. He recognized her. He gasped.

Their horrified faces made her laugh. That hurt.

I must look a sight. Bloody, cut, barely breathing. Nothing like the Dr. Steele they know. I can't look human, in fact. I don't feel human, either. But I'm alive. Thanks to you, my friend. She put her good hand on Guinness's head, lying on her thigh. The dog hadn't moved since she'd dropped Angel. Emma scratched behind her ears.

Angel had gone to the angels.

Don't think so. She was playing for the other team, poor soul.

Police arrived. The first policeman, a heavyset man she'd never met, had questions. Emma had trouble answering.

She had trouble speaking, in fact. Her lungs were not behaving. Everything hurt, from the top of her head to her toes. She could hardly breathe.

"She needs to go to the hospital. Now," Joe said.

The policeman hesitated.

The door flew open. Victor burst in.

"I thought it was a mistake! They said they dispatched an ambulance to this address. I was sure it was a mistake!" He kneeled in front of her, arms open to hug her. He looked at her battered body and didn't dare hold her. He stroked her cheek.

"Emma!" he sobbed.

"She needs to go, Dr. Storm," Joe said.

Victor stepped back.

The door opened. Zagarian burst in.

"Emma! Are you all right? I heard the radio. They said it was a crime scene! I knew it was a mistake!"

She hadn't seen him in weeks. Months ago, they were getting close; then Emma got cold feet and stopped returning his calls. He stopped calling.

Now there he was, impeccable as ever. His perfect gray suit made Victor look shabby in his jeans and dog-chewed jacket.

"I'm fine, thank you," Emma said, even though she was anything but.

"Really?"

She shrugged. The pain in her back made her groan.

"I see." He walked to Angel. He kneeled and felt her neck for a pulse. None.

"An unwelcome visitor, I take it?"

"It's a long story."

Joe was losing his patience.

"We need to take her to the hospital. Now."

"We'll block the door when we're done," the policeman said. "This is a crime scene, we need to work it up."

Emma nodded. The EMTs lifted her on the stretcher. Guinness stood, ready to follow.

"You can't come, sweetheart. I'm sorry. Taylor will be back tomorrow."

"I'll take care of her," Victor said, bending over to kiss Emma's forehead as he patted Guinness's head.

"Thanks."

The officer came closer. "The dog comes with us."

Victor turned, facing him. "Don't touch the dog."

"This dog has killed a person. He's going with us."

"Don't touch the dog. She saved my wife's life."

Moving casually, Zagarian came closer.

"She's not your wife. Not anymore."

Victor looked at him. They'd known each other since February. They worked together to put away a killer, letting Emma off the hook. They stared at each other.

Victor stepped back.

"I'll take the dog."

Zagarian nodded.

"Her name is Guinness," Emma said, as they wheeled her out.

85

Two days later, when she made it home, Taylor looked around in disbelief. Her bedroom looked like a war zone.

Why?

She came for the baby.

That crazy woman came to take her baby. She failed to cut it out of her in the utility room, so she came back looking for her.

Taylor shivered. Eric put his arm around her shoulders, pulling her closer. His touch gave her strength.

That was the worst day of my life.

She had thought that many times before—when her dad left, when she decided to abort, when she found out that Dick had betrayed her, when Eric left.

Nothing like this.

Lying down, unable to move, watching that woman bring a scalpel to her baby.

Nothing. The terror of those moments would follow her to her grave and beyond.

Knowing she was dying wasn't fun. Seeing her baby getting killed was beyond any badness she could imagine.

The last thing she saw, before her mind faded to black, was her mother. Her mother was there. She was going to put it right.

As always, she had.

She woke up thinking about the baby. Was it alive? She welcomed the OB with her ultrasound machine. They looked at the baby together. The heart was beating. The baby moved.

It was alive.

"Does it look normal?" Taylor asked.

The OB doc took a long time. "Two arms. Two legs. Hands. Feet. Spine. Brain. To the best that I can say right now, it looks OK. We should test for genetic anomalies. We'll have another look in a week. For now, I don't see anything bad."

Taylor cried and cried. The OB couldn't understand why.

Eric cried with her.

It was good to be home. With Emma in the hospital, Taylor had the house to herself. The mess that the house was. She had to get it together. Somehow.

What would Mother do?

"OK. Let's get it together. Eric, you go shopping. We need something to eat. I'll clean."

"I don't want to leave you alone."

Guinness barked.

"Alone? What are you talking about? I'm right here!"

86

The hospital drove Emma crazy. She drove everybody crazy too. She climbed out of bed to fix the back support.

A missing screw. She replaced it with a paper clip.

The door opened.

"If you were a dog, you'd be a border collie," Victor said, helping her out from under the bed and handing her an armful of flowers. "You always need something to run after."

Emma smiled.

"If you were a dog, you'd be a Labrador. You haven't met a sofa you didn't like."

Victor laughed and sat in the chair by the bed.

"Touché. We should talk to the administrators about the furniture. I could do with a sofa right here. How are you?"

"I'm OK. They say they'll let me go tomorrow."

"They must be exhausted after caring for you."

"They are. Like all doctors, I make an awful patient. How are you?"

"I'm OK. Taylor's good too. She told me to tell you: 'Don't worry, everything is under control.'"

Emma shuddered.

"I know. I looked around; it looked OK though."

"Guinness?"

"She took her back. I wanted to keep her, but she said absolutely not."

"For someone who didn't want a dog, she surely changed her mind."

Victor laughed. "She didn't not want a dog. She wanted you to have more than a dog."

"I know."

Victor gave her a long look. "And?"

Emma smiled. "How's Amber?'

Victor sighed. "She's good. Busy as usual with the girls and work and her friends and..."

"She thinks you're too busy to spend time with her."

"Really? What makes you think so?"

"She told me. She'd like more time with you. You're always busy. She worries there may be something else happening. Somebody else."

Victor gave her a speculative look.

Emma recognized it, even though she hadn't seen it in ten years. It was the signal for foreplay. She laughed.

"Oh no. Don't even think about it."

He laughed. *Sort of.*

"You sound like my mother."

"That's a compliment!"

"She's sending her love. She said don't forget what you discussed, it still stands."

Emma laughed. "I won't."

"So..."

"No. Give Amber my regards."

Victor bent over to kiss her.

The door opened.

A large bouquet of yellow roses came in, followed by Zagarian.

The men measured each other.

"Come in," Emma said. "Victor was just leaving."

Victor nodded and left. Slowly.

Zagarian took his seat.

"How are you?"

"OK. They're letting me go tomorrow. You?"

"I'm good."

He crossed his legs. He realized he forgot to give her the roses. He lay them on top of her. Emma laughed.

It's good I'm not dead, but if I was, this would make a good start...

He rubbed his chin. "You were right. All the boxes checked. She did murder her father. He was full of morphine. Odd for somebody who refused pain medications. Carlos's potassium was 11. It was normal only that morning. She must have injected him with potassium. His heart stopped. She couldn't use fentanyl, since he was already on the vent. Stopping his breathing wouldn't have done much."

"How about my orders?"

"She logged in the system under your name. For a few bucks, you can buy an RFID copier on Amazon. She copied your ID. That allowed her to document under your signature. Same with Carlos.

Emma shivered.

Zagarian continued: "By the way, we checked New Hampshire. She was involved with Umber. She got into a fight with another nurse, Joy. Joy was fired. Faith followed Umber here. She also dragged Carlos. He found out and ditched her. The rest you know.

Emma nodded.

"What a tortured mind. She said her men refused to have her children. When she found out Taylor's baby's father was Umber, she lost it. She thought Taylor was having her baby. She decided to take it back."

"That's the most horrific story I've ever heard." Zagarian shuddered. "Thank God you were there."

"Yep," Emma said. She looked at the cast on her right hand, the bandage on her left arm, the bandage over her left chest, where the chest tube used to be. She looked like leftovers.

"Thank God I was there."

She looked him in the eye and asked: "Guinness?"

He smiled. "She's OK. We'll call it 'justifiable use of force in self-defense.'"

Emma sighed. "Thanks!"

"Thank her. Emma, I have two tickets to a jazz concert next Saturday. Want to go?"

"I..."

The door opened. A large bouquet of white roses came in, followed shortly by Dr. Roth.

"May I come in?"

Emma laughed.

I wonder if I'd get that many flowers for my funeral. Probably not. Just as well I'm not dead then.

*S*he's back. She smells awful. Like hospital crap, and disinfectants, and iodine, and sickness. But... there's something.

I check her left pocket. I stick my nose in it.

She laughs. She takes out a strip of bacon.

"There. I thought you'd like that better than flowers."

Not bad for hospital food. Salty and smoky. Not crispy. Got soggy with sitting in the pocket and whatnot. No crunch, but hey —two out of three ain't bad. I inhale it. More?

No more.

The girl comes out of her bedroom. She looks at her. Her eyes start tearing.

I growl.

"She looks like shit, I know, but you don't need to tell her!"

She sobs.

"Come on, girl! She's home! She's alive! She brought bacon!"

She stares at Shaman, her shoulders slumped, her belly sticking out.

Shaman sits up straight. She hurts. I smell it. There's a freeze where tears should be. She doesn't do tears, this one. I won't tell.

"Hi Taylor. How are you?"

"I'm OK. You?"

"I'm good. Thanks."

The girl turns around and leaves the room. Like, really?

Shaman slumps. No more need to save face. Nobody here but me.

She looks at me. I put my head on her thigh. She tries to scratch me with her right hand. It's not working. The cast is in the way. The left is better.

"Thank you, Guinness," *she says.*

I don't know what to say. I just did my job. That's what I do. I lick her hand to tell her it's OK. I look up. Her eyes are suspiciously shiny. Not tears, no, she doesn't do that. I get up and lick them. She laughs. Good noise. I like that.

I lay next to her, enjoying the scratching. She's a good scratcher! No, scratch that! She's a great scratcher. Maybe the best I've ever...

The door opens. The girl's back.

"I got this for you." *She brings a bottle.*

Shaman reads. "Brunello de Montalcino..."

Her face drops. Tears start running down her cheeks. I get up to lick them. It's embarrassing. It's only wine, people! If it's no good, just open another bottle!

The girl opens the bottle. She pours a glass. She hands it to Shaman. The girl lifts the bottle. Shaman lifts her glass. They knock.

Shaman takes a sip. She swishes it around like she's brushing her teeth. She swallows it and smiles.

"That's beautiful, Taylor. Really lovely. Thank you."

"Thank you. I wouldn't be here if it wasn't for you."

Shaman shrugs.

"We already knew that..."

"I'm serious. Thank you for saving my life. Even more, thank you for saving my baby."

"It's my job, Taylor. I'm here for you." *She smiles.* "It was also my pleasure. Well, sort of..."

She takes another sip.

"How did you choose this wine? It's spectacular."

Taylor smiles. "I asked Father to get it for you."

"Oh."

"No worries. He told me. I also spoke to Grandma."

"What did he tell you?"

"He said that we all sleep in our beds the way we made them. He made his wrong, but he'll sleep in it."

"Good."

"What will you do, Mom?"

"Frankly, I have no idea. But that's kind of fun for a change. And you? What will you do?"

"The baby seems all right."

"Good."

"Dr. Crump said they'd be happy to have it."

"Yes."

"Eric said it was up to me."

"I see."

"What do you say?"

"I say wait and see. You've grown like crazy over the last few months. There's no hurry to make a decision. Wait and see what feels right when the time comes."

"That's what I was thinking."

"So you 're going to change your mind, since I've said the same thing?"

"Maybe. Have we ever agreed before?"

"Not that I recall."

I bark.

"Enough with this shit. Let's go for a walk."

They stare at me and laugh.

"Well, maybe about this dog," *Taylor says.*

"You didn't want a dog."

"I didn't. But I want this one."

"You can't have her. She's mine."

I bark.

"Get on with it, will you people? I need to shit!"

"She disagrees. As far as she's concerned, we're hers."

ABOUT THE AUTHOR

Rada Jones was born in Transylvania, only ten miles from Dracula's Castle. Growing up between communists and vampires taught her that while humans may be fickle, one can always depend on dogs and books. That's why she read every book she could get, including the phone book – too many characters, too little action – and took home every stray she found, from dogs to frogs.

After immigrating to the US to join her husband, she pursued a medical education and then worked in the ER for years. However, she still speaks like Dracula's cousin.

When night shifts became too much, she left the ER to write. Her ER Crimes series feature serial killers, some nicer than others, and Dr. Emma Steele, an ER doc with a dark sense of humor, a moody daughter, and a love for wine. If blood and gore turn you on, check out <u>OVERDOSE</u>, <u>MERCY</u>, and <u>POISON</u>. If you're into dark humor, check out her medical essays in <u>STAY AWAY FROM MY ER</u>.

But if you're into dogs, the K-9 series is right for you. It started when Rada's beloved German shepherd, Gypsy, crossed the rainbow bridge. To bring her back, Rada wrote her in MERCY. Emma adopted Guinness, a quirky bacon-loving K-9, who took over her life.

Then Guinness insisted on telling her own story. When her friends followed, the K-9 HEROES series was born. BIONIC BUTTER is on preorder. Viper's story is on its way.

To sign for updates, check out RadaJones.com. To get in touch, email her at RadaJonesMD@gmail.com.

facebook.com/radajonesmd

twitter.com/JonesRada

instagram.com/RadaJonesMD

bookbub.com/profile/rada-jones

AFTERWORD

Thank you for reading my book. I hope you enjoyed it. The story continues in POISON, Book 3 in the ER Crimes series.

Fans of Guinness: check out her story, BECOMING K-9, a bomb dog's memoir Book 1 in The K-9 Heroes series. It's lots of fun!

Find excerpts in the following pages. Enjoy!

To get in touch, and for more of my writing, updates and goodies check out RadaJones.com. I'd love to hear from you.

POISON: EXCERPT

"Put me down. Put me down, you motherfuckers. I'm gonna kill you all. Every one of you. I'm going to stab you in your sleep. Put me down!"

The kid was tied to the stretcher, his hands cuffed in front of him. The EMTs pushed the gurney. The police officers walked behind, their heads low.

Really? Cuff a kid? What's he? Nine? Ten? That looks like overkill.

Judy came in just as Emma finishing sewing.

"The kid."

"Yes."

"We need to sedate him."

"Will he take a pill?"

"No. He ripped apart the mattress. He's now hitting his head against the wall.

"Give him 5 of Haldol IM. Make sure he's not allergic."

Judy left. The closed door muffled the screams, making them even more eerie.

"Let me go, you fuckers. I'm going to kill you all. And your babies. And your mothers. And your cats."

The Haldol didn't touch him. He peeled the paint off the walls, put it in his mouth, then spit it against the door.

"This young man has issues," Emma said. "What happened at home?"

The police officer was a former EMT. "Hello, Dr Steele. His mother called us. He killed the cat."

"He killed the cat?"

"Yes."

"How?"

"He stabbed her with a knife."

"Wow! That's different."

"Not for him. Last week he set the dog on fire. He poured gasoline on him and lit him up."

Emma felt sick.

"The mother called us because he threatened to kill the baby."

The urge to vomit became overwhelming.

"Excuse me." She rushed to the bathroom to splash cold water over her face. *Something is wrong with this kid. No normal kid would set the dog on fire or stab the cat. What the heck do I do with him?*

The speakers called her before she could figure it out.

"Dr. Steele to Room 1. Code 99. Code 99 Room 1."

The code in Room 1 looked familiar. She leaned over to see him better.

"It's yesterday's drunk driver," George said, looking up from the IV he was placing. Joe continued CPR.

One hour and many procedures later, the patient was still dead. Police came.

"I thought you took him into custody?" Emma asked.

"We did. They let him out yesterday."

"Why?"

He shrugged. "The judge did. His lawyer got him out on bail."

After he left, George and Emma looked at each other.

George shrugged. "God's work."

"I don't know, George. It's getting hairy. I'm not that religious. It's hard to believe that, suddenly, God decided to fix our community. We need to look into what's happening."

George disagreed. "We're not the police. It's not our job." He glanced around, checking that nobody listened. "Listen, this guy already killed two people—his mother, and the kiddo the other day. Maybe the kid's mother too. We don't even know yet. He was a danger to society. The world is better without him."

Emma couldn't disagree, but she couldn't pretend that nothing had happened. The screams coming out of Room 6 reminded her. The kid. He had set the dog on fire, stabbed the cat, and threatened to kill the baby.

What if the world was better without him too?

BECOMING K-9: EXCERPT

Who knew training humans was so hard? You'd wonder why. They aren't that stupid. It takes them a while, but they eventually learn when you want out, you're hungry or you're thirsty. They can even talk to each other by making noise with their tongue. How weird is that? Even my brother Blue, who's the slowest of us all, knows that the tongue is for lapping water and panting to cool down.

Mom cocked her head and licked my nose.

"That's the best they can do, dear. They have no tails, their ears don't move, and most don't even have enough fur to raise their hackles. No wonder they're confused and need us to guide them. And that's what we do; that's our life's work. But we need to choose them carefully."

Mom was on her sixth litter and very wise. Beautiful, too, with her long muzzle, amber eyes, and smooth, shiny fur, all black but for her golden legs and loving pink tongue.

She glanced at Yellow, who chased his tail instead of paying attention, and growled. He hung his head and sat in line with the rest of us to listen.

It was a lovely summer day as Mom homeschooled us in

Jones's front yard. The warm wind tickled my nose. I bit it, but I caught nothing. I tried again, but Mother threw me a side glance, so I closed my mouth and sat still.

"Boys and girls, today's the day. People will come to check you out and choose which one to take home. They don't know it, but it doesn't work that way. You choose your humans, but choose them wisely. Sniff them all, then pick the ones that smell like food if you want a good life. You may sometimes get bacon, maybe even grapes. Humans say dogs don't eat grapes, but that's poppycock. They just want to keep them for themselves. My grandma was a pure-bred Alsatian, and she loved Riesling. I never had Riesling, but Concord isn't bad."

A shiny strip of drool dripped from Mom's mouth. She licked it off and inspected us. We were seven: three boys and four girls. But that doesn't much matter when you're just ten weeks old. The only difference is how you pee. The boys don't know how to squat so they need something to lift their leg to, like a bush or a mailbox. How stupid!

"Why don't you just lift your leg, if that's what you need to do? What does the bush have to do with anything?"

Mom bristled.

"Leave them alone, Red."

I tried, but it was hard. I was the runt of the litter, so I had to prove myself all the time. Mom said I had a Napoleonic complex.

"What's that?"

"It's when you're the smallest, so you have to be meaner to show them that size doesn't matter."

I told you Mom is brilliant. She came all the way from Germany when she was just a pup. Our human, Jones, has two passions: German shepherds and history. Mom was his first German shepherd, and he spent lots of time teaching her things most dogs never heard about.

He still does, even now that she's old. He sits in his recliner and reads to her as she lays by the fireplace. Sometimes I listen in. There was a story about a dude named Hitler. Not a nice guy, but for loving German shepherds. Another one about that short guy Napoleon who tried to conquer the world while wearing funny hats. And one about some place called Afghanistan.

"That's a bad war, Maddie," Jones said, scratching the four white hairs in his beard. "Those Taliban, they are not nice people."

He calls her Maddie, but her real name is Madeline Rose Kahn Van Jones. He is Jones. The Van is for Van Gogh, some orange dude who got so mad he bit off his own ear. The rest is just for show, since people pay more for dogs with long names; they call that a pedigree. Mom's pedigree is longer than her tail.

As always, Mom was right. People came to see us, and they brought their spouses, their kids, and even their dogs to check us out and choose which one to get. Like, really? Jones said that only one out of twenty German shepherd owners is smarter than his dog. I don't believe it. I bet he fudged the numbers to feel better. You think you own a dog? Who feeds who? Who cleans after who? Who does the work, everything but making decisions? You, human, in case you didn't know it. You don't buy a dog; you hire supervision. But I digress.

My littermates and I wore colored collars so humans could tell us apart. There was no need, really, since we were all different, but humans couldn't see it. What color did I wear? Red, of course. I was small, but I was the queen of the litter, whether the others liked it or not.

A fat man in a Hawaiian shirt stopped to stare at me. He called his female.

"Look at this red one! Isn't he cute?"

She hobbled closer, leaning on her crooked stick. I love sticks, so I tried to take it. She didn't want to let go, but I insisted. They laughed.

"Let's get him."

Jones cleared his throat.

"Red is lovely, indeed, but she's a very active little person who needs a lot of attention. How much time do you plan to work with her every day?"

"Work with her?"

"Yes. Walk her, train her, and play with her."

They stared at him like he'd lost his marbles. He smiled.

"May I recommend Brown here? He's lovely, easygoing, and eager to please. He'll be happy to lay on the sofa watching TV. Or Miss Green? She's a polite little lady who gets along with everyone and never disappoints."

Brown left. So did Green, Yellow, and even White, while I stayed, waiting for my forever home.

"Take it easy, Red dear," Mother said when there were only two of us left—Black and me. "You need to soften up a bit; otherwise, you'll be left without a family. People look for easygoing dogs to fit into their lives, not for somebody to take charge. Though maybe they should, really, but they aren't smart enough to know that."

Her German accent made her words feel harsh. Have you ever listened to Germans? It's like they're constipated while they also have a cold. They keep clearing their throats, so their words come out like bullets from a machine gun. I don't speak German, but I love watching old war movies with Jones.

"What do you mean, om? What should I do?"

"Lick their hands, sweetheart. Wrap yourself around their feet and stare at them like they hung the moon."

"Are you serious?"

"Of course."

"But they're stupid!"

"Come on, Red, don't be so judgmental. You're just a pup, and you have so much to learn. A nice family will give you a good life. They'll love you, play with you, and spoil you. Knowing you have a good, safe home will lift a weight off my soul."

You think I listened? You've got to be kidding.

That's how I ended up in the military.

Made in the USA
Middletown, DE
01 September 2021

47410652R00194